30 Days
of
No Gossip

30 Days of No Gossip

STEPHANIE FARIS

ALADDIN M!X
New York London Toronto Sydney New Delhi

ALADDIN M!X
Simon & Schuster Children's Publishing Division
1230 Avenue of the Americas, New York, NY 10020
First Aladdin M!X edition March 2014
Text copyright © 2014 by Simon & Schuster, Inc.
Cover illustration copyright © 2014 by Annabelle Metayer
Book design by Jessica Handelman
All rights reserved, including the right of reproduction
in whole or in part in any form.
ALADDIN is a trademark of Simon & Schuster, Inc.,
and related logo is a registered trademark of Simon & Schuster, Inc.
ALADDIN M!X and related logo are registered trademarks of Simon & Schuster, Inc.
Also available in an Aladdin hardcover edition.
For information about special discounts for bulk purchases, please contact
Simon & Schuster Special Sales at 1-866-506-1949 or business@simonandschuster.com.
The Simon & Schuster Speakers Bureau can bring authors to your live event.
For more information or to book an event contact the Simon & Schuster Speakers
Bureau at 1-866-248-3049 or visit our website at www.simonspeakers.com.
The text of this book was set in Adobe Caslon Pro.
Manufactured in the United States of America 0214 OFF
2 4 6 8 10 9 7 5 3 1
Library of Congress Control Number 2013944077
ISBN 978-1-4424-8282-1 (hc)
ISBN 978-1-4424-8281-4 (pbk)
ISBN 978-1-4424-8283-8 (eBook)

For Neil,
who always believes in me

Acknowledgments

Dreams do come true. . . . I'm living proof. I wrote my first novel twenty years ago, and it has been a long, adventurous journey.

I have to first thank the person who has been with me longer than anyone—my mom. She's my biggest supporter and my best friend, and I know I will always treasure our daily gossip sessions over lunch. Only when a girl grows up does she fully realize how wonderful her mom is.

You wouldn't be reading this today if not for my agent, Natalie Lakosil. She's more than an agent . . . she's a cheerleader. Her hard work led me to my wonderful editor, Alyson Heller, whose positive attitude and encouraging comments make it so easy to sit down at the computer every day.

My characters come alive thanks to the young people in my life. My stepdaughter, Cambryn; my niece, Hollis; and my nephew, Rhett, remind me what it's like to be young, and they serve as great inspiration for everything I write.

Lastly, I must thank the man who is there for me every day—Neil. It took me thirty-eight years to find you, but it was worth every minute.

Chapter One

Maddie Evans's definition of "gossip":

/ˈgɒsɪp/ Information people want to know, in order to keep everyone aware of what is going on. Information is given by someone who is "in the know"—and that someone is me.

The key to being a good gossip is timing. You have to get the story before anyone else and tell everyone you can *before* it becomes news.

I'm always the girl who knows first. As editor of the *Troy Tattler*, Troy Middle School's unofficial gossip newsletter, I consider it my job. I get the scoop, write it up, and hand it out in front of the cafeteria before school. My BFF, Vi—short for Vivienne—thinks I'm just asking for trouble. She prefers to stay to herself. But I can't help but notice she always sticks around whenever I have news to report.

"Kelsey is mad," I said at lunch. Sydney and Jessica were hanging on my every word. Vi was spooning applesauce into her mouth while pretending not to listen. "Kelsey told Emma in secret that she likes Aiden, but now everyone knows."

"Wait," Jessica said, setting down her roll. It landed on her tray with a *thunk*. "Who likes Aiden?"

"Emma," Sydney interjected. She rolled her eyes and turned back to me. "Go on."

"Actually, Kelsey likes Aiden," I continued. "Emma told everyone. That's why Kelsey's mad."

I didn't add the words "keep up" because that would be rude, but *sheesh*. Did I have to draw a road map for these people?

Ooh, what a great idea! I grabbed my pen, opened my notebook, and hastily jotted an idea for a cute drawing in the next issue of the *Troy Tattler*. Maybe it could even become a regular thing. A gossip cycle. I could draw arrows and cartoon stick-people to illustrate the whole "Kelsey likes Aiden who likes Sarah who likes Trevor" thing. I'm not a very good artist so I might need to get someone to help—

"Maddie?"

That was Sydney, calling me back to earth. I slapped my notebook shut, set my pen on top, and turned my attention back to my tuna sandwich. We were allowed only thirty-five minutes for lunch, so I had to make it count. That meant I had to squeeze at least one piece of gossip in between each bite of sandwich.

Today I'd have to take smaller bites.

"So what's the deal with the field trip?" Sydney prompted.

Oh, that. I chewed as quickly as I could and swallowed. I needed a drink of water, but I had to get this one little bit of info out first.

"It's still on, but Kelsey's sitting at the back of the bus."

Vi shook her head. I saw it out of the corner of my eye. She had to do that, though. It was her job. I gossiped and she played the disapproving best friend. It had been like that since elementary school.

That, in a nutshell, was why Vi and I were so good together. Our moms were neighbors at the hospital when we were being born. I guess the whole thing bonded our moms to each other because they became BFFs in the way moms become BFFs, which basically means they get together every weekend and talk about mom stuff while telling us to go outside and play so we can't hear what they're saying.

Anyway, Vi and I ended up being like sisters. So even though she's quiet and shy and not at all into being part of the whole gossip thing, she's still the best friend I've ever had. Besides, being friends with me means she gets to hear everything that's going on before anyone else.

"How on earth do you find out all this stuff?" Jessica asked. I could hear the awe in her voice.

I shrugged. "I'm good" was all I said. That's all they needed to know.

The truth was, all I did was listen. You'd be amazed what you can find out just by watching and listening. Most of the time people are surprisingly unguarded about what they say, especially when they are upset. I could stand at my locker and overhear six juicy conversations without even trying.

"So." Vi broke in, drawing everyone's attention to her end of the table. "Is everyone ready for the math midterm?"

Midterms. The very subject I didn't want to talk about right now. It was the biggest exam so far that year and I'd done my best to study. But I'd also been working on the *Tattler*, which meant splitting my attention between studying and writing gossip. So, the answer was no. I wasn't ready.

"Yeah, yeah, whatever," Sydney said. "I want to know what Kelsey thinks sitting at the back of the bus on the way to Four Cedars Park will do. Aiden will be in the front with Sarah—"

"And Emma," I broke in to say.

"But Aiden likes Sarah," Sydney corrected.

"Sarah's taken."

Vi was the one who said that. We all turned to look at her.

She sighed and set her sandwich down. "Sarah's going out with Trevor Finn." She looked at me. "Remember?"

Of course I remembered. It was the first piece of gossip I'd delivered to the school at large. It was the very thing that had given me the "queen of gossip" title for which I was now unofficially known.

I'd found out about Sarah and Trevor the same way I found out about everything: I paid attention. It was at the spring social, where everyone was more interested in what kind of ice cream was being handed out than what was going on in the bleachers just a few feet away. But I was watching. Toward the back of the bleachers, I saw Sarah and Trevor talking and holding hands when they thought no one was looking. By the next morning, thanks to me, Sarah Dooley and Trevor Finn were officially a couple.

I consider it a favor, really.

"Can we get back to the exam?" Vi asked, even though she had to know none of us would want to talk about math when the subject of Trevor Finn, the number-one cutest guy in seventh grade, was so much more interesting.

"I say we get on the bus before Trevor does and get a seat near him," Jessica suggested.

"How can we do that?" Sydney asked. "He's not on there yet, so we won't know where he'll sit. Right?"

She looked at me for that last word. I should have an answer for that. They'd expect me to know some dirt on Trevor at this point. I didn't have anything on him. I made a mental note to try to catch up with him after fifth period to see if I could overhear anything.

"Easy," Vi said.

Again, we all turned to look at her. She was chattier than usual today. I figured this time she'd start talking about math again.

"Maddie and I have been riding the bus with him since first grade," Vi began, frowning at her sandwich before setting it down, folding her hands in front of her, and looking at us. "Based on his past behavior, he'll sit in the front two rows. We'll be safe by staying in the third row. The second row would be too far forward."

See? Math.

After a long, awkward silence, Jessica took a deep breath and continued. "So what's the deal with Travis Fisher?"

That loud gulp we all heard came from Vi's direction. Jess and Syd turned to look at her, but I kept my gaze firmly planted on the two of them. They weren't supposed to know Vi liked Travis. It was the one secret I'd been pinky sworn to since third grade, when he'd rescued her lunch sack from the hands of a couple of bullies and become her real-life superhero. I had a feeling Jessica and Sydney had figured it out, though. The way Vi was always staring at him all moony eyed when he passed, they'd have to be blind not to have noticed.

"I don't know anything about Travis Fisher."

They both turned and looked at me. Hey, at least I'd taken their attention from Vi. Now I had to scramble to come up with something else to say.

"I heard he might be kicked off the football team." Jessica shrugged. "He has to pick his grades up in history or he's—"

"History," Sydney added. They both giggled.

I glanced over at Vi. She was good at disguising what she was thinking, which was completely the opposite of me. People could read my thoughts right on my face. Kimberly Browning had told me that about Travis in first period, but I'd been keeping it to myself. My goal had been to tell Vi at the right time, but I guess it was too late now. Jessica and Sydney had delivered the bad news in their own cutesy way.

At the end of lunch, Jessica and Sydney took off ahead of us out of the cafeteria, giving me a few much-needed minutes alone with Vi. I had to get a feel for what she was thinking before I rushed off to my next class; otherwise, it would be bugging me for the next hour.

"You okay?" I asked as we tossed our trash into the nearby garbage and wove our way through the exiting crowd.

She broke into a smile and nodded.

I stopped walking and turned to stare at her. "Wait, you're happy?"

She nodded again, this time even more enthusiastically. Maybe there was some other piece of news I'd missed. I waited for her to clarify. In typical Vi style, though, she just kept walking with that big cheesecake-eating grin on her face. I'd have to dig it out of her.

I chased after her, following her through the cafeteria

doors and out into the hallway. If there was one thing I could do well, it was dig information out of people. But Vi wasn't like ordinary people. Vi was secretive.

All the way to her locker, I tried to get it out of her. She was still smiling, but not talking. I tried guessing, begging, and reminding her that I was her best friend in the whole wide world. Finally it became clear. I'd have to go for bribery.

"Fine," I snapped, crossing my arms over my chest and leaning against the locker next to hers. "I'll help you with your room."

I knew that would do it. Vi lit up. She turned and looked at me, her eyes all sparkly.

"Really? You'd do that?"

She seemed to realize what she'd have to do to get me to do that and deflated a little. Not completely, though.

Decorating was important to Vi. You could say it was her hobby, like the *Troy Tattler* is my hobby. She somehow turned decorating into smart stuff, though, carefully calculating every square inch of her bedroom and drawing exactly what she'd be doing with that inch. It meant so much to Vi, helping her with her room would be like her writing a column for the *Tattler*.

I felt a little stab of guilt that I was only offering to help

Vi to get some info out of her. But, seriously. We're talking weeks of listening to words like "geometric design" and "optimized space." Compared to other people, I was average, but compared to Vi and her ten-ton brain, I was completely clueless.

"Okay," she agreed. "I'll tell you. But you can't tell anyone."

There was a reason Vi said things like that. One of the downsides of being the gossip queen of Troy Middle School was that sometimes I got the feeling that people didn't want to tell me things. Actually, it wasn't even a feeling. People stopped talking when they saw me walking by, and even my friends—the people who were supposed to trust me more than anything—would start to say something, look at me, and clamp their mouths shut.

Which is why I had to be extra good at eavesdropping.

"I don't tell anyone anything you tell me," I told Vi. That wasn't entirely true and she knew it. I just hoped she wouldn't point out the time I let it slip in front of everyone in gym class that she still slept with her childhood teddy bear.

Luckily, she was too caught up in her excitement to worry about that. She closed her locker and leaned in close to tell me her secret.

"I figure it's like this." Vi's voice was barely above a whisper. "Travis is off the football team, right?"

I nodded, even though we weren't sure about that. Sometimes you just had to go with a rumor.

"If he's off the team, I might have a chance," Vi said. From the look on my face, she probably got that I wasn't following. "He might like me back."

I looked around. The halls were crowded, reminding me just how hard it was to stand out around here. It didn't help that Vi was so shy. She barely talked to anyone but me. Any friends I had became friends of hers, too.

There was no way Travis would just start noticing her, even if he *was* off the football team.

Which was silly, because Vi was pretty. Even a popular guy like Travis Fisher *would* like her. If only he knew she existed.

It was like a lightbulb went on inside my head. *That is my job.* As her friend, it was my *duty* to get through to Travis for her.

I knew she'd freak out if I told her I planned to say something. But I could already imagine the look on her face when I told her he liked her too. At that point, she'd forgive me for giving her secret away.

Chapter Two

"I KNOW SOMEBODY WHO LIKES YOU."

Travis was in my sixth-period class. I'd like to say he just happened to sit next to me, but I actually had to cross two aisles and pass three people just to get to him.

As he stared at me, his eyes wide, I started having second thoughts. It wasn't too late, I told myself. I could just go back to my seat and leave him wondering who liked him. He probably wouldn't chase after me later to find out.

That was exactly what I planned to do when I stood and started walking away from him. I was halfway to my seat when Travis called out to me.

"Who?" he yelled. "Who is it?"

Everyone was staring at me at that point. I had to say something. Sure, someone else might just give him a mysterious look and let him keep guessing, but I remembered the reason I'd walked over here in the first place. Vi. I imagined how excited she'd be when Travis liked her back. They'd go out and I'd be the best friend who had made it happen.

Even though everyone had stopped staring, it was still important to keep this as quiet as possible. I returned to Travis's side, knelt down, and whispered, "Vi Lakewood."

His face scrunched up and he squinted at me. "Who?"

I should have expected that. I tried her full name. They were in second period together, so he'd probably heard his teacher call her by that.

"Vivienne Lakewood," I whispered.

Nope. That one didn't register either. He shook his head and continued to stare at me like I was from another planet.

Even though I was friends with some of Travis's friends, we'd never really spoken before. He was definitely cute. Cute guys made me nervous, especially when they were waiting for me to say something.

"She's really pretty," I said loudly, realizing only after I'd said the words that I was no longer whispering. I lowered my voice again to whisper, "You'll see me with her in the hall after this class."

She always rushed this way when class let out . . . mostly to walk by Travis. But he didn't need to know that.

I knew I should stop talking, before I said something I'd regret. Sometimes I needed someone to slap a piece of duct tape over my mouth.

Once I was safely seated across the room from Travis, I started to get excited about seeing Vi again. She'd pass us in the hall, Travis would look at her as if seeing her for the first time—and she would *know* he liked her. I just wanted everyone to be happy.

The bell rang and I sprang for the door, as usual. It was important that I got to Vi before Travis caught up with us. I had to be with her so Travis would know who she was, decide she was the most beautiful girl he'd ever seen, and fall madly in love with her. Or something like that. I wasn't sure what Vi wanted out of this, since she was so secretive about things, but I was guessing that would be just fine with her.

"Are you coming over today?" Vi asked without even saying hi. We wove around the throngs of people rushing toward the exit to catch buses, keeping our pace quick until we got close to where we'd run into Travis. That was when we slowed down and I acted as though it were completely normal for me to be walking this way when I'd just left class.

Any other day, Travis wouldn't have even glanced our way, so it was no big deal. I figured this was just something

I did for Vi, as her friend. If it made her happy, I'd do it. But today I saw him looking through the crowd, trying to find the girl I'd told him about.

His gaze landed right on her. I watched for an expression and saw his eyebrows lift. He liked her.

Didn't he?

That was how I interpreted it. If he'd frowned at her or wrinkled his nose in disgust, that would be bad. But an eyebrow lift had to be a good thing. Like he was surprised to find how cute she was.

Or surprised that she was smart and talented and had other things to worry about besides how she looked.

I shoved that last thought aside and grabbed Vi's arm. "Look!" I squealed.

Vi winced. Squealing wasn't really her thing. She probably hadn't squealed once in her life. Squealing was *my* thing, though, and this was my good news.

Instead of looking in Travis's direction, she turned her glare on me. "What on earth . . . ?"

"He's looking at you," I blurted, smiling as I pointed at him. I actually pointed. If there was one thing you didn't do to Vi—besides squeal—it was point at the boy she liked while he was looking your way.

Only, he wasn't looking our way anymore. He wasn't

even standing there. So what I was pointing at was Kathina Freeman, who saw me pointing and took it as her cue to come rushing toward us.

"You're Vi, right?" she asked, stepping in front of us. She walked backward to keep up, despite the fact that she was in serious danger of running into one of the many people rushing in the opposite direction of us. "I told Travis I knew who you were."

Oh no. This wasn't good. I'd told Travis quietly. It wasn't possible anyone had overheard. Unless . . .

I looked over at Kathina, my eyes wide. She sat directly behind Travis, but I didn't think she'd been there when I gave the news to Travis. Travis must have asked Kathina if she knew who this Vi person was.

"That's so cool that you like Travis Fisher," Kathina, totally missing my warning stares, continued. "My best friend likes him too. Do you know Chelsea Tucker?"

Chelsea Tucker was one of the most popular girls in seventh grade. She had long brown hair with red streaks and perfect skin and everyone thought she was beautiful. If she liked Travis, Vi didn't stand a chance.

Vi was looking at me. *Uh-oh.* For once the look on her face told me exactly what she was thinking. It wasn't good.

"I need to speak with you a second," I told Vi, grabbing her arm to pull her away from this blabbermouth. "Come on."

Vi was going nowhere. In fact, she'd come to a dead stop in the center of everything. Two people almost ran into her and someone yelled something at her, but Vi didn't notice any of it. Her stare was firmly fixed on me.

And it wasn't a happy stare.

I had two choices. I could run as far and fast as my feet would carry me, or I could face this. Running away wouldn't fix it. I wasn't sure talking to her would fix it either, but I had no choice. I had to try.

Unfortunately, Kathina was still standing there. As was her friend Robyn. And another girl had joined her too, but she had to be in another grade because I didn't recognize her.

"Can we talk?" I asked Vi. "Alone?"

"No," she said. *What did you do?*

"I just thought Travis should know—"

"That was our *secret*." Vi stepped closer to me. She was speaking quietly, as though she didn't want any of these people to hear, but of course they could hear. They were listening to every word of this.

"Excuse us," I said to Kathina and company.

Kathina and Robyn looked at each other, shrugged, and walked off. The other girl stayed.

"You too," I added. I didn't know her, so I didn't have to be nice.

Vi didn't wait for the stranger to be completely out of earshot before saying, "I asked you not to tell anyone, and you told . . . everyone?"

"Not everyone. Just . . . Travis."

My voice drifted off on that last word. Vi was too busy going ballistic to hear me.

"You told Travis? *Travis?*"

That last part was a shriek. Luckily, the halls had already cleared out, so no one could hear us. But that also meant we both were probably going to miss our buses, which meant I'd have to start making up with her fast so I could talk her into getting her mom to come pick both of us up. Otherwise, I'd have to call Mom at work, and she would not be happy.

"Just listen," I said. "He likes you back. I'm sure of it."

That didn't get the reaction I'd thought it would. She didn't light up or smile or anything. She just stood there, frowning at me, her arms holding her books protectively in front of her chest.

"He didn't know who you were at first," I admitted. When I saw her frown deepen, I rushed to add, "So I told him we'd be walking together after class."

She narrowed her eyes. "You told Kathina Freeman," she accused. "You told everyone."

"He told Kathina, I guess. He must have asked who you were."

Why did I get the feeling I was just making things worse? There was only one thing I could say that would even have a chance of making her less angry. I decided to go for it.

"He lifted his eyebrows," I said.

She didn't get that, at all. That much was clear right away. She seemed to tighten her grip on those books as she edged backward. She was creeping away from me. I had to say something to keep her there.

"When he saw you," I explained. "He lifted his eyebrows like this."

I demonstrated the exact look Travis had gotten on his face when he saw Vi. Okay, so maybe I exaggerated a little. I made it look like a "wow, she's the most beautiful girl I've ever seen in my whole life" reaction instead of the "maybe I think she's cute" expression I'd really seen.

It didn't help. Vi had known me long enough to see through stuff like that.

"He really did lift his eyebrows," I repeated. "I think he likes you."

It took me saying that to figure out that Vi didn't care about Travis's reaction. This wasn't about whether he liked her or not. It was about me giving her secret away. I'd been wrong. Even if Travis had walked up to her and asked her to go out with him, she still would have been mad at me.

"I'm . . . sorry?" I asked sheepishly. Too little, too late. She was getting angrier by the second, I could tell. If she were a cartoon character, steam would be coming out of her ears.

"You have a problem," she said.

I opened my mouth, waited for something to come out, then closed it again. That would have been the last thing I would have expected her to say. I didn't know what to say back. I couldn't argue with her, because I had to make up with her, but I didn't agree with her either, even though I knew exactly what she was about to say.

"You can't stop gossiping," she told me. She was backing her way toward the entrance of the school. I was following. I'd trail her all the way out the door if that was what it took. "You can't stop being the star for a second."

That last sentence almost brought me to a halt. I had to walk fast to keep up with her, though. A star? Who said I wanted to be a star? I just liked being the one who knew everything and could tell everyone first. It made people like me. It made me popular.

"You don't remember what it was like back in elementary school, but I do," Vi continued. "Girls like Kathina and Chelsea Tucker were the ones everyone liked. Now everyone likes you. They come to you to find out what's going on. You couldn't stand for that to stop, could you? You care too much what everyone else thinks."

I shook my head. No way. That wasn't true at all. I didn't care what anyone thought. Sure, it was nice to have so many people give me shout-outs as I walked down the hall, and I was friends with just about every group of people in my grade, no matter how popular or unpopular. I didn't want that to go away, but that wasn't why I gossiped.

And yes, I remembered elementary school. I remembered third and fourth grade, when Vi and I played by ourselves during recess because nobody else wanted to talk to us. I remember being nicknamed Fatty Maddie because I had extra baby fat that, luckily, disappeared by fifth grade. And I remembered sitting with Vi at lunch, watching Kathina, Sarah, and Chelsea giggling as all the other kids gathered around to tease the rest of us.

Over the years, I'd learned a few lessons. When you had secrets, people wanted to be around you. If you could entertain people with imitations and funny stories, they liked you even more. So I used my observations to create entertaining stories. It wasn't bad. Everyone did it!

"I just think it's important to tell the truth," I said. "That's why I publish the *Troy Tattler*. People need to know things."

Vi had reached the front entrance by then. She pushed the front door open with her butt and stepped out into the sunlight. Car riders were standing beneath the sign, waiting for parents to pick them up. Since Vi and I were supposed to be bus riders and neither of us had called our moms, I knew we had time.

"People want privacy," Vi continued. "You take that away from them."

That wasn't true at all. Was it?

"I think we should stop being friends," Vi told me.

The gasp escaped my lips before I even knew it was about to happen. "We aren't just friends. We're sisters, remember?"

That was what Vi and I had said when we were younger. We'd even introduced ourselves to people as sisters. With moms who were best friends, and with the amount of time we spent together, we pretty much were. Sometimes we went on vacation together and stayed at each other's houses all weekend.

We couldn't stop being friends, especially not because of something stupid I'd done.

Vi had stopped walking backward by then and was standing just a few feet away from all the car riders. She faced me with a cold, hardened look on her face. This wasn't the Vivienne I'd always known. I'd never seen her so angry. Did I just lose my best friend?

"I'll be your friend on one condition," she said finally.

"Anything."

I tossed the word out before I considered what she might ask of me. It could go far beyond just asking me to apologize for telling Travis she liked him.

She waited several seconds, drawing out my agony, before finally blurting out the two words I never wanted to hear. "Stop gossiping."

Chapter Three

IT WAS IMPOSSIBLE. I COULDN'T DO IT.

Vi didn't just want me to give up gossip. It would mean I'd have to stop writing the *Troy Tattler*, stop telling anyone anything about anyone else. It was pure craziness.

"But . . ."

I'd been about to argue that if I didn't write the *Troy Tattler*, who would? Halfway through the sentence, though, I'd thought better of it. Arguing would just make it worse.

"Thirty days of no gossip," Vi added. "No newspaper, no talking about other people, even Sydney and Jessica."

Our closest friends? It was easy for me to tell her I could do it, but what about when some juicy piece of gossip came my way? How would I keep that to myself? Could I do that for thirty days? Thirty days wasn't too long . . . was it?

"You know what, forget it," Vi said, noticing the look on my face. She turned around and nudged a girl who lived two houses down from her. "Can you give me a ride?"

"I'll do it," I yelled out.

Vi turned back to face me. "It was a stupid idea. You won't be able to pull it off. I know you. Gossip is your life."

"You're my best friend." I sounded sad, even to myself. "Our friendship is far more important to me than the *Troy Tattler* or gossip. I can do it."

And I meant it. It was just thirty days. Thirty days was nothing compared to *forever* without Vi.

"It's silly," Vi said. "Forget it. Forget the whole thing."

"No," I insisted. "Let's do this. I can do this." I wasn't sure who I was trying to convince more, myself or Vi.

Vi narrowed her eyes, stepping toward me again. "Are you sure? Because I have ways of finding out if you slip up."

"You won't have to find out," I assured her. "If I agree not to gossip for thirty days, we'll stay best friends, right?"

It was important that I clarified that. I didn't want the thirty days to be up, only to find we were back to her being mad at me.

She considered for a moment. "Yes," she said. "If you can pull this off . . ." She looked sad for a moment. "Then you'll still be the best friend I've always had. But only if you agree not to gossip," she ended firmly, losing the sad look. "No more talking about people or telling people's secrets."

I wanted to argue that what I'd done had been to try to help her. I wanted to argue that I would never give one of her secrets away unless I thought it was in her best interest. I wanted to point out that sometimes it was necessary to give away someone's secret if they were, say, getting themselves in trouble or missing a great opportunity. Like finally getting the boy they'd liked forever to notice them.

I wanted to say all of that, but I knew it was pointless. I just needed to agree to whatever Vi asked and work out the rest later.

Vi's neighbor leaned forward to say something before taking off toward a car. Vi turned back to me.

"My ride's here," Vi said. "So we have a deal?"

I nodded. "Thirty days of no gossip. Deal."

But it didn't hit me until Vi was gone, leaving me standing there alone with no ride home. *Thirty days of not telling anyone anything.*

It probably wouldn't fully get through to me until I saw something important I wanted to tell people about. But I had to do it. Vi was the best friend I'd ever had, and I couldn't sit across the room from her, knowing she wasn't speaking to me *because* . . . of gossip.

* * *

By the next morning, I already missed gossiping. But I missed Vi more.

When we made our deal, we weren't clear on whether or not she'd be speaking to me during those thirty days, but I had my answer by the next day. She hadn't taken any of my calls—and we were used to talking at least an hour a night—and she didn't meet me to walk to the bus together.

So I showed up for school early to stand next to her locker.

I considered it a bad sign that she walked right past me and started working her locker combination. After thirteen years, it had come to this? Vi pretending I didn't exist while I begged for her attention?

"You aren't speaking to me?" I asked.

Silence. I was aware at this point that I looked like a total stalker, but I didn't care. I leaned against the locker next to hers and talked like nothing had changed.

"You can't go thirty days without speaking to me." She said nothing. "We're sisters." Silence. "I told you I'd go thirty days without talking. If you ignore me, how will you know whether or not I didn't gossip for thirty days?"

Still nothing.

I decided to appeal to her the only way I knew how. "We took vacations together, remember?" I gave her a second to respond, and when she didn't, I added, "We had that contest to see who could collect the most seashells?"

She closed her locker and started walking. I chased after her. I realized I probably looked like a crazy person, trying to talk to someone who wasn't even looking at me, but I didn't care. If I had to go thirty days without talking to my BFF, I'd die.

"Could you just agree that you'll talk to me as long as I don't mess up?" I asked. "I'll give you permission to stop speaking to me forever if I mess up."

She didn't say a word, just stared straight ahead, her jaw clenched. She was mad. I could tell from the look on her face. I assumed she was still mad about the whole thing I'd done with Travis. But she had to forgive me . . . right? That was what friendship was all about.

I decided to try something different. "Are you ready for midterms?" I asked, rushing to keep up with her. I had no idea she could walk so fast. "All studied up?"

No answer. I began to get an uneasy, desperate feeling. I thought I might even feel myself breaking into a sweat.

"We have our field trip tomorrow," I blurted, my voice

all tight. "I thought we'd sit together on the bus and hang out. All our friends are the same."

No matter what excuse I threw her way, she just kept walking. It was like I was invisible or something. I wasn't invisible to anyone else in the hallway, though. I had to rush around them as they grunted and gave me looks. I didn't care. Until I got Vi to talk to me again, nothing else really mattered.

"Hey, guys."

From out of the crowds of people gathered in the hallway stepped Sydney, smiling at us like it was any other day. She fell into step next to Vi and leaned around her to include me in the conversation.

"You won't believe it," Sydney gushed. "Kelsey just stomped past Emma and Aiden. OMG. It was epic. *Epic.* I can't believe you missed it. I think Emma and Aiden might be going out."

I opened my mouth, dying to say the words that were now stuck in my chest. Seriously, that's how it felt. Like a ball of words stuck in my chest that I couldn't get out. I wondered if someone could get really sick from holding words in like that. Maybe even die. Vi would feel really bad if I died from my chest being all clogged up with words, wouldn't she?

I looked over at Vi, who glanced my way for the first time. *Don't do it,* her eyes said. *Your chest will come unclogged on its own.* Okay, so she didn't know about my chest being clogged, so that wasn't possible, but she did know I wanted to say something.

It wasn't like I even wanted to gossip. I was just going to correct Sydney and let her know that Emma didn't even like Aiden. It was Kelsey. So if Emma was hanging around Aiden, chances were she was just talking about how much Kelsey liked him and that was really sweet of her. She was trying to help—like I'd been trying to help Vi yesterday when I spilled the beans to Travis Fisher.

I couldn't say any of that, though, because it was considered "gossiping." Which was really messed up because I wasn't doing anything more than correcting her. But I realized that with what Vi had asked me to do, even standing here listening to Sydney might be against the rules.

"What?" Sydney asked, looking from me to Vi. She must have sensed all the tension. "What's going on?"

"Nothing," I said. "Vi's just . . . mad at me. Right, Vi?"

Vi gave me a look. Hey, progress. Two looks in less than a minute. They were both mean looks, though, so I wouldn't count them.

"Why?" Sydney asked.

Vi came to a stop and turned to face Sydney, which meant her back was facing me. I moved around her so I could be a part of this too.

"It's a long story," Vi replied. "And it's between the two of us. Nobody else."

"I can't talk about it." I flashed a grin at Sydney, even though the last thing I felt like doing right now was smiling. "Are you ready for midterms?"

Sydney looked over at Vi. It was a "Is she for real?" look. She probably thought I'd lost my mind or something to be asking about midterms. I never talked about studying or schoolwork or anything like that. If Vi brought it up, I always changed the subject to something more important.

Like shoes.

Or clothes.

Or who liked whom, who was going out with whom, and who was mad at whom.

"Who cares?" Sydney asked. "Didn't you hear what I said about Kelsey and Emma and Aiden? This is big. *Huge.* How can you talk about tests at a time like this?"

I took a deep breath and blurted, "If you can't say something nice about someone, you should just keep your mouth shut."

I'd heard that saying before, but not in those exact

words. It didn't matter, though. Sydney just stared at me.

But this wasn't about what Sydney thought of me. This was about avoiding gossip without letting anyone know I was avoiding gossip. I knew, as well as Vi probably knew, that if I told people I couldn't gossip anymore, they'd freak out.

No more *Troy Tattler*. No more catching everyone up on what was going on with everyone else around here. I'd be talking about schoolwork and other things that would make everyone yawn. Pretty soon nobody would want to talk to me or sit with me at lunch, and I'd be stuck sitting there alone, remembering the days when everyone liked me.

Gossiping was just so much fun.

For just a second I let my mind wander. Vi wasn't talking to me anymore, anyway. So when Syd and Jess called, what would stop me from talking about whatever I wanted to talk about? It wasn't like Vi would have bugged my cell phone or something. Syd and Jess wouldn't run to her right away to tell her I was gossiping. The only way she'd ever know was if someone passed along what I'd said and Vi overheard.

The two sides of me battled it out for a second, but in the end, I knew the answer. I had to stop gossiping. I couldn't lose Vi as a friend forever, not only because she was like a sister to me but also because she balanced me out. If I didn't have Vi around, I'd just sit around saying bad things about people, looking for ways to pick everyone around me apart. I'd be left with only Sydney, Jessica, and all the other people in school who rushed toward me to say bad things about other people. With all that negativity, eventually I'd become a horrible person.

The kind of person my mother would be ashamed of.

Besides, I could do this. How hard could it be . . . really?

Chapter Four

The Troy Tattler

By Maddie Evans

If I could gossip, I'd tell you
that Aiden Lewis told Emma Mayfield
he might like Kelsey O'Dell. She
likes him back but she's still mad
at Emma, so Emma can't tell her the
good news. I can't tell you the good
news either, because I can't gossip.

Teacher gossip I can't tell you:
Mr. Boucher was out sick last
Friday and all his classes had
subs. But if he was sick, why did a
student on vacation spot him at the
lake, tossing his fishing pole into
the back of his truck late Friday

> afternoon? Too sick to come to
> school but not too sick to fish?

"Maddie!"

My mom's voice jerked me out of my internal gossip fest. I knew exactly why she was yelling for me. I'd heard the phone ring while I was typing, but I didn't want it to be for me. If it was for me, that could mean only one thing—

Sighing, I reached over and grabbed the phone on the nightstand next to my bed. I had a cell phone, but my friends never called me on it because my parents bought me a phone that had, like, six minutes of talk time a month or something. I used it for sending gossip texts and checking social networking sites for any new news.

"Hey, Mads."

I held in a groan. Just as I feared.

"Hi, Syd."

"What'cha doin'?"

"Studying for midterms," I lied. Well, it was only partly a lie. My history textbook was open on the bed next to me, but my laptop was on my lap. I'd been busily typing away on a *Troy Tattler* I could never, ever show anyone, but I figured it didn't count as gossip if nobody ever heard or saw it.

"I thought you might be getting ready for tomorrow," she said.

"What's to get ready?" I asked, sounding more like Vi than I ever had in my life. "I'll just throw something together in the morning."

Sydney's gasp was so loud, it was as if she were sitting next to me. "You'll just 'throw something together in the morning'?" I could almost see her gaping jaw. "I have to know what you're going to wear."

She *had* to know. Was it gossiping to tell her? I thought about it a minute and decided probably not. Gossiping was talking about other people, right?

"My red T-shirt and some jeans."

"The ones with sequins on the back pockets?" she asked.

I nodded, then remembered she couldn't see me. "Yes."

"Good. What do you think Vi will wear? Do we need to call and tell her to wear something that fits?"

I winced. Granted, Vi wasn't a fashion plate, but she had far more important things to worry about than clothes. She was on the honor roll because she spent time studying instead of trying to figure out what to wear tomorrow. That was a good thing. We all should be like that. Plus, Vi could make a normal bedroom look like something out of a magazine, so I was pretty sure that if she really cared about it, she could outdress every single one of us.

I realized I couldn't even stick up for her. Not without gossiping. I clamped my mouth shut. Again, I had that feeling that I was holding in words. Maybe I should just stay away from talking to people for the next twenty-nine-and-a-half days.

"I'm sure she'll wear something cute," I said, biting my bottom lip nervously as soon as the words were out. I was so confused about what was gossip and what wasn't, I wasn't sure what to say anymore.

"I'll call her and tell her what we're wearing," she offered. "That should take care of it."

"Don't!"

I didn't mean to yell into the phone, but I could already picture the conversation in my mind. Sydney would call Vi and tell her that she and I had just talked and decided tomorrow we'd be wearing our sparkly jeans and red tees. Vi would deem it "gossip" and stop speaking to me forever.

Maybe not, but I couldn't risk it. "I'll call her," I rushed to say. "I'll see you tomorrow."

"Wait," I heard her say as I was reaching for the button to hang the phone up. "I wasn't finished talking."

Another suppressed groan. I'd figured as much. She'd

want to talk. And talking meant gossiping. And even if I listened to gossip, I could get in trouble. Even one "uh-huh" could be heard as agreement.

"What are we going to do about Trevor?" Sydney asked.

"What do you mean?" I asked. I wasn't playing dumb this time. I really had no idea.

"The bus," she said, sighing.

Oh, yeah. The whole bus thing. Trevor was supposed to sit at the front of the bus and Kelsey would be at the back, pretending she didn't like Aiden. The plan had been that we'd sit up front, where Sarah and Trevor would be sitting, all hand-holdy and stuff, while Aiden stared at Sarah with puppy-dog eyes like he always did. We were supposed to watch the action, I guess. But now that I'd overheard someone saying Aiden had told Emma he might like Kelsey back, all of that had changed. I wasn't even sure Aiden would sit near Sarah.

Of course, I couldn't say any of that. I had to hold it all in, along with all the other words that were backed up inside my chest. This was a lot harder than I'd thought.

"We can just sit in the middle," I finally said. "No big deal."

"No big deal?" Sydney asked. "No. Big. *Deal*? Who are you and what have you done with Maddie?"

Uh-oh. Busted. How was I supposed to deal with this? Nobody had told me how to deal with this.

"Gotta go," I rushed to say. "My mom's calling."

I hung up the phone without waiting for a response and tapped in Vi's number as quickly as possible. She had a cell phone too, but hers had unlimited minutes. Since she wasn't much of a phone talker, that was kind of a waste.

No answer. Of course. Why had I thought there would be? I hung up the phone around the time it went to voice mail and stared at my laptop screen. What if I IM'd her? Would she reply to me then?

I decided it was worth a try. I opened my instant messenger and started typing.

"Hey," I typed, my fingers moving quickly over the keys before I could lose my nerve. "I know you're, like, mad at me and all and not speaking to me, but I think Syd's onto us."

I waited, watching the blank white screen, which seemed to burn my eyeballs. It said Vi was online, but it always said that. She had it set so people couldn't tell if she was offline, idle, or typing away, so nobody could bug her when she didn't want to talk. She was kind of antisocial when it was exam time.

I waited a few minutes more but got no response. I

chewed my lip thoughtfully for a while. I imagined her across the room from her computer, not even looking in that direction. The Vi I knew would be furiously studying, buried in her work, only seeing her IMs later tonight, maybe right before she went to bed.

If that was the case, it wouldn't matter whether she responded to me or not. I could say what I had to say and she'd read it and think about it. So I thought for a second longer before I started typing again.

"We were talking about the field trip tomorrow, and she noticed I wasn't gossiping," I wrote. "She asked who I was and what I'd done with Maddie. People are going to start to notice I'm not gossiping. I think we should tell them about our deal."

I sat back, rereading what I'd typed. If I knew Vi, she wasn't even thinking about the field trip. She'd jump out of bed and head to school in the morning like it was any other day.

That was when it hit me. I didn't have to tell people Vi had made me not gossip. I could say I was trying to be a better person. It was my own idea. Still, people would freak out if they knew they couldn't get information from me anymore. They'd try to talk me into gossiping and try to make it harder. It would be better if I could just change the subject whenever someone tried to get me to gossip. They'd probably bug me about it, but they wouldn't make me gossip.

The answer came to me while I was staring at that blank instant-message screen. I had to figure it out myself. That was part of it. Vi wanted me to be a better person and to stop gossiping altogether, not just for thirty days. I knew that much. And if I was going to be the person she'd dared me to be—the person she thought I never *could* be—I had to learn to find a way to handle everyone throwing gossip at me without having her talk me through it.

The phone next to my bedside rang, scaring the bejeebers out of me. I slammed the laptop shut and looked at the caller ID. Part of me thought it might be Vi, calling to talk to me about what I'd sent her. I knew better than that, though. If she did start talking to me again, it wouldn't be because I'd IM'd her to tell her people were asking why I wasn't gossiping anymore.

It wasn't Vi. It was Jessica.

Deal with it myself. Okay. I could handle this. I picked up the phone and took a deep breath before blurting out a cheerful, "Hello."

"Well. What's with you?"

That wasn't a good sign. The conversation hadn't even

started yet, and already I was setting off Jessica's "Maddie isn't acting like herself" alerts. I had to come up with something that wouldn't mean the end of the *Troy Tattler* but would still explain my sudden change in personality.

That was when it hit me. It was the perfect idea.

"Just trying to be more positive," I announced, smiling at the brilliance of my idea.

"It's about time," Jessica said. "Life's too short to always be so grumpy."

I started to agree before I realized what she'd said. "Hey!" I objected, sitting straight up on my bed and staring grumpily at the phone.

"No offense," she said.

"I don't think I'm that grumpy." I caught my reflection in the mirror across the room, saw my frown, and immediately forced it into a smile.

"Whatever." Jessica paused a minute, then continued. "Are you going to tell me what's going on or what?"

I immediately tensed. Sydney had no doubt called her immediately after our conversation. The two of them talked to each other almost as much as they talked to me. Most of the time, they called me just to find out what I knew so they'd have something to talk about when they called each other.

"With what?" I asked, stalling for time.

"Tomorrow," Jessica said. She didn't sigh, but I knew she wanted to. "The field trip?"

This had been the same conversation I'd had with Syd a few minutes earlier. I wanted to talk about it. I wanted to gossip about what Sarah Dooley would be wearing and how we thought Kelsey would react if Sarah sat near Aiden. Instead, I asked the only nongossipy question I had.

"What time are we supposed to be there?"

"Huh?" Jessica asked. I knew I'd only get away with those kinds of questions until Jessica started talking again. "I don't know. Check your e-mail. I'm talking about the whole Kelsey-Aiden-Sarah-Trevor situation."

"I don't want to talk about this."

"Since when don't you want to talk?" Jessica had a panicky, are-you-crazy tone to her voice. I had to pull the phone away from my ear to save my eardrum.

Great, Maddie. Now get yourself out of this one.

"I'm trying to be more positive, remember?"

I wasn't sure that one would work or not, but it was worth a try. If they asked, I'd tell them I'd been watching some show on TV about positive thinking and how it can fix all the problems in your life.

"Talking about someone's crush *is* positive," Jessica said.

"It's like we're reporters. It's our responsibility to know what's going on."

I was beginning to feel a little trapped. There would be no way out of this but to admit I couldn't gossip, but if I did that, they'd try to talk me out of it. They might even do everything they could to get me to gossip again. There was only one thing I could do.

"Gotta go," I said, the words rushing out of me. "My mom needs me."

Chapter Five

THE FIRST THING I NOTICED AS I RODE UP TO THE school on my bike Saturday morning was that there were no kids out front. It was early, but we'd been told to get here early to leave for the field trip. Shouldn't other seventh graders be gathered here for the field trip?

The front of the school wasn't completely deserted, though. As I drew closer, I squinted at the strange shapes that were far too tall to be anyone who went to this school. Grown-ups. Three grown-ups I'd never seen before, to be exact. I sped over to the bike rack, locked up my bicycle, and by the time I turned around, they were walking toward me.

"Do you go to school here?" one of the women asked. She wore big dark sunglasses and capri pants with an expensive-looking tank top. Actually, everything she wore looked really expensive. Her hair was perfectly styled and she had a lot of makeup on. In other words, she didn't look like she was from around here.

"Yes," I said. "Are you here for the field trip?"

It was probably a dumb question, but that was the only reason to be here today. The woman in the tank top looked at the two men standing behind her and smiled before turning back to me.

"No, we're here to see Mr. Shelly." Mr. Shelly was the principal. "I was just wondering if you could point us in the direction of his office."

I turned toward the front door of the school and saw a line of cars heading down the street that led to the back of our school. That was where the band room was, as well as the practice football fields. It hit me then.

Our field trip! We were meeting in the back.

"I have to go," I sputtered, rushing off. "The front door to the school is there. Good luck."

I wondered about the three strange people on the front lawn, but only as long as it took me to get around to the back of the school and see the line of people climbing onto the school bus. How had I missed such an obvious instruction? I'd read the e-mail and it had said the time and place, but I didn't remember anything about the back of the school.

There was no point worrying about the people out front, anyway. I couldn't gossip about it, which meant I couldn't even ask anyone what was going on. Someone might have known, but Vi would give me her disapproving frown if she heard me asking about it.

So I got in line behind the last person, craning my neck to see if I could see my friends on the bus and hoping they would save me a seat. After last night, they may have decided I was too boring to hang out with all the way to Four Cedars Park and invited someone else to sit with them.

I should have known better. There, in the third row, sat Sydney and Jessica, with Vi in the seat behind them. That brought me to a stop midway down the aisle. Was that spot for me? If so, did that mean . . . ?

Did that mean Vi was speaking to me again?

Feeling hopeful for the first time in more than a day, I started forward again. I plopped down on the seat next to her like nothing had changed at all. I thought, for a second, she might have been saving this for someone else, but then it hit me that if she were, she couldn't tell me. She couldn't say a word. She'd be stuck with me all the way to the park.

Vi didn't speak. She just kept looking out the window and I wasn't sure she even knew I'd sat down. I faced forward, looking past Syd and Jess. Sure enough, Trevor and

Sarah sat in the row in front of Sydney and Jessica. They weren't holding hands.

"I thought you'd never get here," Jessica said, spinning around in her seat to look at me. "What took you so long?"

I didn't explain to her that I went to the front of the school. I felt like a big idiot, especially compared to Vi, who managed to make it to the right place even though she was absorbed in studying for midterms. In fact, it looked like everyone on this bus had known to come back here. I had clearly missed something.

"I had to park my bike," I told her.

"We could have given you a ride." This from Sydney, who had also turned around to look at me. I wondered if Vi had even said anything to them. Maybe she wasn't speaking to anyone.

"I didn't mind," I told Sydney. Mom usually only let me ride my bike on weekends, when there wasn't much traffic on the roads. During the school week, she was sure some rushed commuter or parent would run over me on the way. But this morning we had to be here early, which meant there wouldn't be much traffic. After I begged long enough, she finally agreed to let me ride it.

"He's in front of me," Sydney whispered back to me. As if I couldn't see.

I nodded. "I can tell." I looked over at Vi for approval. She was staring out the window, but I knew she had to have noticed my silence when I was clearly being invited to gossip.

"Are they holding hands?" Jessica whispered.

I played innocent, as if I had no idea what was going on. "I don't know," I said with a shrug.

Vi still didn't look at me, but I knew she had to be fully aware of what was going on here. She was listening to every word, so I had to be on my best behavior.

Jessica looked at Sydney, who just shrugged. They both turned around to face forward.

I looked at Vi. She was still staring out the window. There had to be some way to get her to talk to me. If I started talking to her, eventually she'd talk back. Or she'd listen, which is all I really needed her to do.

"So . . . ," I began, searching for something to talk to Vi about. What did we normally talk about? I know Vi didn't gossip, but we always seemed to have more than enough to say. I would talk about things going on at school, maybe whatever was happening with Sydney and Jessica. Most of the time, I was talking and Vi was listening. I glanced at Vi out of the corner of my eye. Now that I thought about it, Vi rarely said anything at all. I just chatted away while she listened.

"Are you ready for midterms?" I asked.

Her head jerked around. She leaned over and dug into her backpack, which she took everywhere with her. Once she even took it to a water park with my family. We had to get a separate locker just for her.

Without saying a word, she pulled out her notebook and set it on her lap. My comment about midterms had reminded her to study. That was good news because it meant she was actually responding to something I'd said, even if it wasn't to say a word. But it was bad news because it meant she planned to study the whole way there.

Studying? Really? The ride to Four Cedars was more than an hour. If she studied the whole way, I'd have no one to talk to. I needed someone to talk to even if she would never say a word back.

I looked at Syd and Jess in front of me, their heads pressed together as they whispered and giggled. I wanted to be up there, laughing along with them. No, scratch that. I wanted to laugh and whisper with my BFF. I just had to find a way to get back to the great friendship we'd once had without gossiping.

The idea came to me as I watched her do mathematical formulas in the left column of the page of her notebook. It wasn't my first choice of things to talk about, but it would make her happy.

"We could talk about your bedroom," I tried. It was a sad attempt to get her to talk to me, I knew.

Her hand completely paused. She'd heard me. She was listening. I continued.

"This is the perfect chance to go over our plans," I said. "You know. Your interior design project."

She started writing again. I took that as a sign she'd heard me.

"Pssst."

The sound came from just behind me as I was in the middle of coming up with a way to get through to Vi. I was sure the noise wasn't for me, but I couldn't keep myself from turning around.

I saw Kelsey O'Dell standing in the aisle, looking at me, Kelsey, the girl I'd been gossiping about with my friends before Vi banned me from gossiping.

"Can you come back here?" Kelsey asked.

Kelsey and I hadn't spoken since third grade, although I'd certainly said plenty *about* her. So if she wanted me to move to the back of the bus, I could only assume I was in trouble for something.

"Excuse me," I said to Vi. She didn't even look up, but I still felt like I should excuse myself. I would have felt really bad if she'd kept talking to me when my attention was on

Kelsey. She *was* drawing what her bedroom would look like with all her furniture rearranged, which meant she'd been listening to me.

I got up and headed after Kelsey, moving as quickly as I could to avoid being caught moving around by the driver. I had a bad feeling about this, but what could I do?

Kelsey wasn't all the way at the back of the bus. Just seven rows behind us, actually. She motioned for me to sit down next to her as she slid onto the seat. I hoped this didn't mean we were settling in for a long conversation.

"What do you know about Sarah Dooley and Trevor Finn?" Kelsey asked.

I don't know why I was surprised. This should have been exactly what I expected her to say. If Sarah and Trevor were still a solid couple, she'd have nothing to worry about. If, however, they were having trouble, it might start a chain reaction that went all the way down to Kelsey. If Sarah was free, she might finally realize Aiden liked her and like him back, at which point Aiden's whole thing about *maybe* liking Kelsey would be over. And Kelsey would have a good reason to be mad at Emma.

Just like Vi would have a good reason to be mad at me if Travis ended up with someone else.

So in this situation, Kelsey was Vi. I had to talk to her

the way I'd want someone to talk to Vi. I had to get her to be not mad at Emma. And I had to do it without gossiping.

Yeah, *that* would be a challenge.

I took a deep breath and plunged in. "Emma's your best friend, right?" I asked.

That wasn't gossip. It was a fact. Plus, it was a question, so that made it double-not-gossip.

"She was," Kelsey said, pursing her lips until they made an almost straight line. "Until she told Aiden I like him."

Treading carefully, I started, "Sometimes best friends do things to help each other. We really just want to help."

"She knew I didn't want her to say anything," Kelsey said angrily. "I feel like it's a betrayal." She shook her head, as if shaking the whole thing off. "Anyway, I want to know what's going on up there. You know everything."

I *knew* everything. A gigantic lump suddenly formed in my throat. She was counting on me to deliver information, but I couldn't, not without betraying my own best friend. After what Kelsey had just said, how could I take that chance? If I even said one thing, I ran the risk of Vi saying the same thing about me. *She betrayed me. I trusted her.*

Best friends keep secrets. They trust each other. Even if it was in the best interest of that best friend, the other best friend should never break that bond, no matter what.

That was how Kelsey felt about it, and that was how Vi felt about it too. I was starting to understand why Vi was so mad.

So I simply told her, "I'll see if I can find out."

Yes, it was a cop-out. It was what I had to say without breaking my promise to Vi. I practically sprinted back to my seat, where Sydney had now plopped down in my place next to Vi.

"What if you put the bed over here?" I heard Syd ask as I passed the two of them. Their heads were bent over Vi's sketch pad, and I felt a twinge of envy. Just minutes ago Sydney and Jessica had their heads bent together like that, gossiping, and now Sydney was doing the same thing with Vi, only not to gossip. Without gossip, I wasn't sure I really had anything to talk about.

I paused next to Jessica's seat as that thought hit me. Was that exactly Vi's point?

"Sit," Jessica commanded.

I looked down and realized she'd probably been looking up at me for a couple of seconds. The bus hit a bump and I had to grab on to the back of the seat to keep from falling over. I sat down next to Jessica.

"Where did you go?" Jessica asked.

That question threw me for a second. How did she

know I'd gone anywhere? I heard Sydney laugh behind me and remembered she'd taken my seat.

"Kelsey wanted to know what was going on up here," I said quietly. I didn't want Vi to hear. Not that I had anything to hide. I just didn't want her to get the wrong idea.

"What did you tell her?" Jessica asked. She whispered too. She probably thought we were trying to keep Sarah and Trevor from hearing. Emma was sitting across from us too.

"Nothing," I answered with a shrug. "I don't know what's going on. Don't care."

That last part may have sounded rude, but I knew if I didn't add it, Jessica would proceed to tell me everything she'd observed. Which was gossip. Vi would overhear her telling me all that, and our friendship would be over.

It didn't matter. Jessica wasn't listening.

"They're fighting," Jessica whispered. "Look."

I looked. I shouldn't have, because that was participating in the gossip. Sure enough, Sarah and Trevor weren't all cuddled together like they normally were. I could see the tension in the air between them. It was creepy.

Here's what I wanted to say: *OMG. What happened? I want to hear every single detail of everything you saw. Does Emma know? Is that why she keeps looking nervously back at*

Kelsey? Because you know if Trevor and Sarah break up, that gives Aiden a chance, which will really make Kelsey mad.

Here's what I said: "That's too bad. What did you bring for lunch?"

Jessica gave me that look. It matched what Sydney had said last night. Who *are* you and what have you done with Maddie? I knew what was coming, so I braced myself for her next words.

"You're being weird."

Those weren't the exact words I'd expected, but they weren't a surprise, either. I just shrugged.

"I told you I'm trying to be more positive."

"You're Maddie Evans," Jessica responded. "If Maddie Evans doesn't talk about people, what does she talk about?"

She didn't say that last part quietly. I looked around, glad to see nobody was really paying attention to us. Vi and Sydney had stopped talking, though. Sydney gave us a half smile before saying something that brought Vi's attention back to her drawing.

"There are lots of things to talk about," I said. "Can you believe how hot it is?"

The weather? *Really?* I couldn't come up with anything better than that?

"I know. We're going to burn up out there."

Those words came from Sarah, who spun around in her seat and looked directly at me. Her eyes were flashing something I couldn't quite read, but from her expression, I knew instinctively she'd figured out people were gossiping about her. She saw my silly talk about the weather as a way to get away from it.

"Pimento cheese," Jessica blurted. We both looked over at her, surprised at her sudden outburst. Then I remembered I'd asked Jessica earlier what she'd brought for lunch. She was trying to cover up the fact that she'd been talking about Sarah by talking about her sandwich.

"We were talking about what we brought for lunch," I lied to Sarah. Well, it wasn't exactly a lie. I'd been *trying* to talk about what we brought for lunch. It wasn't my fault Jessica hadn't been cooperating.

"Cool." She spun around in her seat. "I brought cold chicken."

"Excuse me."

That came from Trevor, who suddenly stood and started toward the back of the bus. The bus driver yelled out that if we didn't stay seated, he would turn around and take us all back to school. At that point, Sarah burst into tears.

My first instinct was to turn to Vi, but her attention was on her drawings. Typical Vi. Major drama was happening right in front of her and she was more interested in what she was doing. At least it had caught Sydney's attention. She was staring directly at Sarah.

I looked at Jessica. She had a horrified look on her face. I gave her a "what should we do?" look, but she was no help. It looked like I was on my own with this.

Sighing, I stood and moved up to sit next to Sarah. We weren't good friends, but we'd gone to school together since kindergarten. I figured if you'd both slept on the same mat in kindergarten during nap time, you had at least a little bit of a bond.

"It's okay," I said, reaching out and touching her arm. That was as close as I could get to a hug. I looked around. People were starting to stare, and I knew later they'd ask me what was going on. "It's going to be okay."

What else could I say? She was crying. I didn't know what to do when people cried.

"He. Broke. Up. With. Me."

Sarah said those words quietly, inserting a sniffle in between each one. She said them so quietly, I didn't think anyone heard them but me. Why was she telling me this, though? She knew I was the school gossip. Didn't she think I'd tell people?

As I watched her wipe tears away and slide down farther

in her seat, it hit me that she probably wasn't even thinking about that. It was just now hitting *her* that other people might see her crying, including Trevor.

I slid down even with her. I tried to think of something smart to say—some little piece of wisdom that would make her stop crying—but I'd never even liked a boy, let alone dealt with a boy not liking me back. Being broken up with had to be far worse than either of those things.

"He's stupid," I said quietly.

Yep, that was it. My big wisdom. I expected Sarah to wipe her tears away and look at me like I was a piece of lint on her brand-new black T-shirt. Instead, she looked up at me and hiccuped.

"You think so?" she asked.

I nodded and smiled. "Here's what I think will happen. You'll meet some really cute boy in a couple of weeks and he'll like you and you'll like him. Trevor will see you together and realize what a big mistake he made, but by then it'll be too late."

She was listening now, in a way people used to listen to me when I talked about other people. This wasn't gossip, though. This was *helping* someone. And it felt really, really good.

"You know what?" Sarah asked, wiping at her cheeks

again before pushing herself up until she was sitting up straight. "You're right. Thanks."

I sat up straight too. "You're welcome."

"Hey." She leaned closer, glancing back nervously before speaking. "Could you do me a favor and not tell anyone about this conversation?"

Chapter Six

I HAVE TO GIVE SYDNEY AND JESSICA CREDIT. THEY waited until we were finishing our hike and finally away from everyone before they started questioning me.

"Was she crying?"

"What's going on? Did he break up with her?"

I was walking next to Vi. She was staring straight ahead, not contributing to the conversation at all. These were the kinds of tests I'd have to suffer through for the rest of the thirty days. And then I would get my best friend back.

"She's fine," I said. "What about that tree over there?"

It was finally lunchtime, and one of our chaperones, Miss Hunter, had told us to find a place to eat lunch. It was so hot, my potato chips were probably melted and stuck together by then.

"You have to give us the scoop," Sydney whispered. We sat down, automatically forming a circle. "We want to know everything that happened with—"

"Sarah!" I called out loudly, mostly to alert Syd and Jess she was coming since they had their backs to her. I didn't mean to sound so happy to see her, but . . . well . . . I *was*. "Come sit with us."

It was obvious that was exactly what she'd intended, since she was walking straight toward us. I just wanted to stop Syd and Jess from asking more questions.

"Is it okay?" Sarah asked, stopping several feet from us and giving us a really sweet look that made me feel guilty for telling our entire second-grade class her dad had left and her parents were getting a divorce.

Not to mention the whole Sarah-and-Trevor-holding-hands thing.

"Sure," I said brightly. "There's plenty of room. Scootch over, guys."

Sydney and Jessica flashed each other a look before shifting to the left to make space between Jessica and Vi. It was like they were doing a weird little dance.

"You okay?" Sydney asked. She sounded concerned,

but anyone who knew her knew she was just being nosy.

"Sure," Sarah said. "Thanks to Maddie, I think I'm going to be fine."

Everyone turned to stare at me. I wondered if I had enough time to dig a hole in the ground and crawl into it. Probably not.

I looked over at Vi, knowing she wouldn't speak but eager to see her reaction. She was staring right at me, her eyebrows arched. Uh-oh.

I could feel the questions coming on. Jessica and Sydney, being all nosy, would try to work in some question about what was going on, and Sarah may or may not tell them. If she didn't tell them, they'd expect me to tell them later.

So I changed the subject. "Where do you get your clothes?" I asked. "You always wear the cutest things."

"You do," Syd added.

Subject successfully changed. I turned to Vi and gave her a "See? I can avoid gossip" look, but Vi didn't look impressed. Instead, she'd pulled a small brown paper sack out of her bag and was rifling through its contents.

"My mom works for McComb's," Sarah told us. "She gets a huge discount, especially when there's a sale. I could see if she could get you guys some things."

Vi lit up, which was weird, since she wasn't all that into clothes. "Can you get a discount on bedroom stuff? Like curtains and bedspreads?"

"Vi's redoing her bedroom," Sydney explained. "And I'm helping."

"Awesome," Sarah said. "Your parents are letting you pick everything out?"

"She has really good taste," Sydney answered.

"I'll see what I can do."

As everyone pulled out their lunches and started eating, I sat there, frozen. Sydney was helping with Vi's bedroom? Since when? That was supposed to be *my* job. Sydney sat next to Vi on the bus for thirty minutes on the way here and talked about Vi's drawings, and that made her Vi's official helper?

And why was it that Vi could talk to them but not to me? I was starting to feel a little hurt.

"Did you see what Miss Hunter was wearing?" Sarah asked suddenly, pulling me from my thoughts. "It looks like she got dressed in the dark."

"I know, right?" Sydney added. "Jess and I were just talking about that. Nothing she wears ever matches."

As they launched into a ten-minute conversation about the various quirks of the Troy Middle School faculty, Vi and I sat silently on the sidelines. Vi seemed focused on her food, which is exactly what I pretended to do. But I was listening to every word they said.

I had to keep reminding myself that none of this could go into the *Troy Tattler*, since the *Tattler* was currently off limits. Even if I typed it all up and made the best *Troy Tattler* ever, no one could ever read it. Still, I hung on every word people around me said, processing it and preparing it for later. It made me feel better, even though I couldn't share it with anyone else.

"Did you know Coach Ryan had lunch with Miss Einhorn?"

"Chelsea Tucker was caught chewing gum in class Friday."

"Maddie said they're doing away with pizza at lunch."

Everyone looked at me, including Vi. *Especially* Vi. Her eyebrows were arched again, only this time she looked annoyed.

"How do you know that?" Sarah asked.

"I said that a couple of weeks ago," I rushed to say. I didn't look at Vi when I said it, but I saw her out of the corner of my eye. "It may not be true."

"So why did you say it if it wasn't true?" Sydney asked.

Before I could answer, Sarah spoke. "Where did you hear it?"

I looked at Vi. Was it gossiping to answer that question? Not if I chose my words carefully.

"I was in line in the cafeteria and I heard the lunch lady talking about it," I said with a shrug. "So, like I said, she may have been making threats."

"How exactly did she say it?" Sarah asked.

Again I looked at Vi. She was watching me too, but I knew this was a test. How I answered this question might make the difference as to whether Vi decided I'd made it through this lunch without gossiping.

"Um . . . I don't remember," I stalled. "You were there, Vi. Do you remember what she said?"

Vi set her sandwich down. "I think it was something like, 'They shouldn't be serving pizza to you kids. If that council votes it down, you'll all be eating broccoli.'"

"The word 'broccoli' was definitely used," I said, flashing Vi a grateful smile. I knew fully well that Vi hadn't even been listening when the woman in the cafeteria had started spouting off about pizza. She'd heard it secondhand from me over lunch that day. And I'd exaggerated it. At this point, I couldn't remember whether she'd mentioned any kind of council voting, but it sounded good.

But that wasn't the important part. The important part was that Vi had talked to me. Well, sort of. Her comments were directed at everyone sitting here, but she'd heard what I'd said and had responded to it. That was closer to talking than we'd come since she'd gotten mad at me.

"I'll just bring my own pizza," Sydney said. "They can't keep me away from eating it."

"You fight that fight," Vi told Sydney. She tossed her trash in her sack and stood. "If you'll excuse me, I'm going to talk to Miss Hunter."

Sarah waited until she was gone to start talking. She leaned forward.

"You don't think she'll tell her what we were saying about her, do you?" Sarah asked.

Was I the only one who was confused? "Who?" I asked.

Sydney and Jessica looked at me like I should know the answer to that one. "Miss Hunter," they said in unison. Jessica spoke alone when she said, "We were talking about her outfit, remember?"

"Oh, that." I watched Vi head toward Miss Hunter, sketch pad in hand. I knew exactly why Vi was heading over there and it had nothing to do with clothing. "She wants Miss Hunter to look over her design ideas."

Sydney's mouth formed into a pout. "I was helping her with that."

"She likes to get advice from different people," I said.

"I don't think she likes us talking about people," Sarah suggested. "She acted all weird when we were talking about Miss Hunter."

"Vi doesn't believe in gossip," I said.

They were all looking at me now as if this were big news. It wasn't. It was just that Sydney and Jessica had spent so many years hanging on my every word, they'd never noticed how quiet Vi was.

"Let's put it this way," I said, knowing that if I didn't say something quickly, they'd probably say something not so nice about Vi and I'd be forced to defend her, which would just make them talk about me when I got up and walked away. "Would you want people talking about you?"

"I'm sure they do," Sarah answered, sitting up straighter. "I'm sure we've all been talked about."

"Vi doesn't want to add to the problem." I shrugged. Then I sat back and finished my sandwich while they all stared at me.

Finally, Jessica spoke. "So what about the *Troy Tattler*?" she asked.

That was the question I'd been dreading. "What about it?" I asked. It was a delaying tactic, but I knew I could put her off only so long.

"Now that you're acting like . . ." Jessica seemed to search her mind for the right word.

"Vi," Sydney supplied.

"*Vi,*" Jessica said, nodding. "Now that you're acting like Vi, you won't be doing the *Troy Tattler* anymore?"

I opened my mouth to answer, but my gaze was scanning the lawn around us, now scattered with kids running and hanging out and tossing paper sacks into garbage cans. I was looking for a distraction when I saw Vi waving toward me. She was calling me over.

"Gotta go," I said, hopping up, gathering my trash as I stood. "I'll see you guys on the walking trail."

We were all going to spend the afternoon hiking to some lake, which would have been great if it hadn't been so hot. But in the meantime, we were hanging out, waiting for Miss Hunter and the other chaperones to start yelling for us all to line up.

As I plopped down next to Vi on Miss Hunter's blanket, though, I couldn't help looking back over my shoulder. They were looking over here. When they saw me watching, all three of them quickly turned back around again.

They were gossiping about me, I just knew it. It felt weird. Sarah's words stuck with me. *I'm sure we've all been talked about.* Believe it or not, as much as I'd talked about other people, I rarely stopped to think about other people talking about me. Now that I thought about it, though, it had to happen. Probably often.

The thought bugged me for the rest of the trip.

Chapter Seven

What's with Maddie Evans?

She used to be Troy Middle's biggest gossip, but lately she's been acting like she's better than everyone else. She keeps walking off when we try to talk to her, and this morning she told Kathina Freeman she shouldn't be talking about people. It wasn't nice. Since when did the queen of gossip become the queen of high-and-mighty?

"Maddie Evans."

I looked up from my cell phone, where I'd been madly typing away into an e-mail that I planned to send to myself. It was this week's *Troy Tattler*, and it was all about me. Not that I'd ever let anyone else see it. I was pretty sure gossiping about myself still counted as gossiping.

Miss Einhorn was staring down her flawless button nose at me. She wasn't standing over me yet, but in just a couple of steps she would be. And she'd see the cell phone I had hidden on my lap. I covered it up with both my hands, but I knew the screen was still glowing.

"Are we interrupting your texting?" she asked.

"I wasn't—"

I realized two words into my argument it was a waste of time. I didn't want to explain what I'd been doing and she didn't care anyway. That wasn't the point. The point was, I was on my cell phone instead of paying attention to her lesson on rational numbers.

"Take it to Mr. Shelly," Miss Einhorn said.

We had a rule at Troy Middle. If a student was caught using a cell phone in class, we were sent to the principal's office without question. There, our phones were taken away for the day, and we were given a stern warning on responsible cell phone use that included warnings against texting at the dinner table and not turning the phone off in movie theaters. Mr. Shelly believed it was important to equip us for life.

At least people would have something to gossip about.

Maddie Evans was sent to the principal's office for texting in class. It wouldn't matter that I hadn't been texting. The gossipers would fill in the blanks with whatever they needed.

I avoided eye contact with everyone in class as I gathered my books and left the room. I didn't even grab the hall pass from beside the door. I figured if someone stopped me, I'd just hold up my phone and they'd know immediately why I was out of class.

I noticed two things when I entered the school office. Nobody was behind the reception desk and Mr. Shelly's door was open. Normally you'd check in with whoever was working the front desk, then sit in one of the chairs to wait until Mr. Shelly came out to get you. I could sit in one of the chairs and wait, but what if Mr. Shelly didn't know I was out there? And what if nobody came back to work behind the desk? I'd be sitting out there forever and lunch period was coming up and I really didn't want to miss that.

So I walked over to Mr. Shelly's door and knocked. It was wide open, but I didn't dare look inside because, let's face it, none of us wants to know what a principal does when he's not principaling. He might be eating a box of Twinkies or something.

"Come in," an unfamiliar female voice said.

So Mr. Shelly had company. It was probably the

woman who normally worked the front desk, bringing him his mail. I stepped inside, ready to explain why I'd been sent here, hand over the cell phone, and get out as quickly as possible.

The first thing I noticed was that Mr. Shelly was nowhere to be found. His chair was empty. The second thing I noticed was that there was someone in the chair normally occupied by kids like me, who'd been caught texting in class.

"I know you," the woman in the chair said. She stood and turned to face me. "You're that girl from Saturday."

I remembered the woman too. It was Miss Hollywood, the girl who had been standing in front of the school Saturday morning. It looked like she'd found Mr. Shelly after all.

"Is Mr. Shelly around?" I asked, looking around nervously. I don't know why she made me feel so uncomfortable. I think it had something to do with how expensive her clothes looked.

"He'll be right back," Miss Hollywood said. "You can sit down here."

"I can just wait outside," I offered. "I'm sure he'll want to talk to you first."

Which meant I'd miss the beginning of lunch period. Which stank.

"No, seriously," she said. "I'm here to observe."

She moved to her chair, gesturing to the empty one next to her. I eyed her cautiously as I moved around the chair and sat down, settling my books on top of my lap and looking at Mr. Shelly's empty chair. I wondered how long it would take him to show up.

"What are you observing?" I asked. I figured if I was the one being observed, I at least deserved to know that much.

She didn't see it that way, I guess. "Just . . . things," she said mysteriously. "I can't really say."

We both stared forward for a minute. Did I have the right to say I didn't want to be observed? Maybe I could make a deal that I would come back after lunch.

Mr. Shelly broke the silence by barreling through the door and around his desk. He was in such a rush, he didn't even see me until he was already seated.

"Oh." He looked from me to Miss Hollywood. Observation number one: Mr. Shelly had no idea who any of his students were. Except maybe the ones who were always in trouble. I was proud to say I wasn't one of those students.

"We have company," Miss Hollywood said. "This lovely young lady . . ." She gestured toward me. She wanted me to say my name. Because she'd called me a "lovely young lady," I said it.

"Maddie Evans," I said.

Mr. Shelly made a thoughtful face. He was trying to place my name, but I was pretty sure he wouldn't succeed. I edited and wrote the *Troy Tattler*, but my name wasn't actually on it. Sure, my friends knew it was me, but I didn't know if the teachers and principal knew about it. I hoped not. If they did, they might have shut it down.

"Well, Miss Evans, Miss Golden and I are in the middle of something, so if you could just wait outside . . ."

I looked over at Miss Golden. Of course that was Miss Hollywood's name. Golden. Just like her hair, her skin, and everything about her.

"That's okay," Miss Golden said. "I'd love to see an interaction between you and one of your students. Go ahead."

She flashed her dimply smile in my direction, which totally put me off track. How could I talk about being sent to the principal's office in front of this stranger, who was watching me for some reason she couldn't tell me?

"Maybe I could come back after lunch?" I asked, looking from Miss Golden to Mr. Shelly.

"Miss Evans, I'm really limited on time right now, so if you could just tell me why you're here, that would be a real help," Mr. Shelly said, rubbing the bridge of his nose.

Fine. I tried my best to ignore Miss Golden as I explained

everything that had happened. Leaving out, of course, the fact that I'd been gossiping about myself on my phone when I was caught with it. Unfortunately, Mr. Shelly wouldn't leave it at that.

"You were texting in class," Mr. Shelly accused. He looked over at Miss Golden. "This is an ongoing problem at Troy Middle School. Kids love their cell phones."

"Sure," Miss Golden said, nodding. "We weren't allowed cell phones when I was in school."

They probably didn't have cell phones when Mr. Shelly was in school, he was so old. I noticed he didn't comment on it.

"At Troy, we put trust in our students." Mr. Shelly turned his pointed gaze on me. "We prefer to teach them responsible cell phone habits."

I had responsible cell phone habits, I wanted to argue. But I didn't really have an argument for this, since I'd been using my phone in math. I nodded. Nodding would get me out of here more quickly.

"Fascinating," Miss Golden said. She leaned forward in her chair, her gaze fixed on Mr. Shelly. "Have you considered a cell phone area? You could even line up phone booths along the wall."

He frowned. No surprise. The day Mr. Shelly allowed a

cell phone area in school would be the same day he lined the halls with vending machines full of junk food.

"I'm afraid that isn't a very wise use of our budget, Miss Golden."

"Call me Ashley," she said. "We could line up tables along the wall with small partitions in between to block out noise. It would be a great little break area for the kids. You'd like that, wouldn't you?"

She was looking at me now, and I had no idea what to say. I was here to get my five-minute lecture on proper cell phone habits.

"I . . . guess." I looked over at Mr. Shelly, who was already ready to move on to his lecture. But Miss Golden was interested in what I had to say. I was a sucker for that interested look.

"Break areas are very important," Miss Golden said, nodding as if confirming her own idea was great. "Kids need break areas. What else would you like to see?"

Wow. This was it. My chance to speak up for the entire seventh grade. It wasn't gossiping, so I could still make a difference without breaking my promise to Vi.

"Maybe it could be used for other things," I blurted, thinking as I spoke. "There could be charging stations if people need them, and if someone has an emergency or is talking to their parents, they could take phone calls there."

I could see Mr. Shelly wasn't happy. He wouldn't go along with this, no matter what, as long as the words "cell phone" were wrapped up in it.

"It could also be extra space for meetings," I rushed to add. I had to get this all out in one big burst or Mr. Shelly might cut me off. Then I'd miss my chance forever. "Everyone meets right after school, and there are never good places. Nobody wants to meet in a classroom, and the gym and cafeteria are already taken. It would be cool to have a meeting place with comfortable chairs and lots of privacy."

In the silence that followed, I could tell that Miss Golden was really considering what I'd said. I held my breath, wondering if she'd say I was a genius and this was the best idea ever and Mr. Shelly should take it to the school board right this very second.

Or maybe not. Mr. Shelly broke the silence by clearing his throat. The sound was so sudden, it made me jump.

"Miss Golden, I think it might be best if Miss Evans and I take care of our business so you and I can work on our project without interruption," Mr. Shelly explained.

"Of course," she said. "Go ahead."

She sat back, waiting for us to pick up our conversation

where we had left off. Only now I didn't remember what I was even here to do. I couldn't stop thinking about what she'd said about a break area. Was she here to somehow . . . make this school better?

But why?

"I think you've learned your lesson," Mr. Shelly said. "You may go."

"Wait," Miss Golden called out. She was digging through her purse, from which she retrieved a pen and crumpled-up receipt. "What is your name again?"

"Maddie Evans," I called back. I was already halfway across the room at that point, my attention firmly fixed on the door. I wanted out before Mr. Shelly changed his mind.

"I may be in touch," Miss Golden said. Then, as I slipped through the still-open door, I heard her say, "I have a good feeling about her."

I wasn't sure what to make of that, but I was smiling as I headed out of the principal's office just in time for the end-of-class bell. At least someone had a good feeling about me.

```
What famous reality show producer
is eyeing Troy Middle School for
possible inclusion on her show?
Maddie Evans has the scoop. . . .
Only, she can't tell any of you.
```

My fingers hesitated, poised above the keys of my laptop. I stared at the blinking cursor on my screen, biting my lip thoughtfully for a second before going back to re-review the search results in my Web browser. If I was going to pretend-write the *Troy Tattler*, I had to at least get my facts straight.

Ashley Golden was not a hard person to track down online. She was on every social networking site, plus she had an official website. Was it gossip if I was only reciting the facts I'd found on the Web?

I knew the answer to that. I knew that no matter how much I learned about that woman in Mr. Shelly's office, I couldn't speak—or write—a word of it to anyone.

If I could write about her, I'd tell the school that Ashley Golden's website—which included a large, smiling photo of her with her dog, so I knew it was her—stated proudly that she was the producer of a show called *24-Hour Makeover*, a show Vi was absolutely addicted to. It was one of a billion reality shows where people came in and redesigned some-thing, but in the case of *24-Hour Makeover*, the redesign wasn't to a house. It was usually to a hospital or library or old, run-down tourist place.

I was no brainiac, but I could kind of figure out why *24-Hour Makeover*'s producer was hanging out with our principal so much. First of all, Troy Middle School was about a thousand miles away from where that show normally filmed, so it wasn't like Miss Hollywood just happened to be hanging out with our principal. Second, this was a school. As far as I knew, they hadn't done a school yet, so it was perfect.

Oh, and did I mention this school was built in the Dark Ages and looked like something out of a TV show my grandparents would have watched?

We were totally going to be on *24-Hour Makeover*! I was dying to tell someone the news, especially Vi. She'd made me watch a billion hours of the show. A picture of its host, Jilly, was taped to her mirror. She would totally die when she found out.

I picked up the phone and started dialing Vi's number, getting four numbers in before remembering I couldn't call her. I put the phone back down and turned to my laptop.

As I prepared to start typing again, my phone rang. Vi? It took me a second to talk myself out of hoping it was her. Since it wasn't her, it didn't matter, so I answered the phone without even looking to see who it was. Instead of Vi, it was Sydney.

"Hey," she said without waiting for me to say hello. "I have Sarah on the line. Tell her."

"Tell her what?" I asked, returning my gaze to my monitor. Just hearing Syd's voice made me want to start typing. I could pour all the things I couldn't say to her into the *Troy Tattler*. It might make me feel a little better.

"About Aiden Lewis," Sydney said. "About how he likes Sarah."

I froze. Not good. Not good at all. Even though Vi wasn't on the line, I could imagine her listening, not daring to move as she waited to see if I'd pass this latest test.

"You'll have to ask Aiden about that," I told her.

Sydney kept speaking as if I hadn't said a word. "But last I heard, Aiden might like Emma. Kelsey likes Aiden, you know. Right, Maddie?"

I was starting to think Sydney was doing this on purpose. She was trying to get me to gossip so I'd be more like my old self. The big question was, how did I get out of this?

Sarah cleared her throat, reminding me she was on the line with us. So I did the only thing I knew to do.

"Sarah, do you like Aiden?" I asked.

There was a long silence before Sarah finally said, "I don't know."

"That's all that matters," I said. "That's all you can control."

"That's pretty deep," Sarah replied, sounding impressed.

"I think you should write about it in the *Tattler*," Sydney suggested. There was a definite challenge in her voice. "Just get it all out in the open. That way Aiden will have to make a decision."

"Maybe," I said, because I had no idea what else to say. I needed out of this conversation quickly. "I was sent to the principal's office."

I blurted that last part out in desperation. I didn't want them to know about my trip to Mr. Shelly's office, but I had to say something. I knew right away that I'd made a mistake.

"What happened?" Sydney asked, her voice full of awe. There was a heavy silence in the air as they waited for me to fill them in on everything. It was something I'd gotten used to back in my gossiping days, but I wasn't gossiping.

Was I?

I was. I had to go. Now.

"I need to do homework," I said quickly. "Talk to you guys tomorrow."

I hung up before they could say anything. While I was at it, I switched the phone's ringer off too. If I didn't do something to avoid my friends, I'd be in trouble for sure.

I returned my attention to the laptop and started typing.

Maddie Evans was sent to Mr. Shelly's
office earlier today when a spitball
fight got out of control in fourth
period. Maddie, a seventh grader who
always has a notebook full of paper
for scribbling down great gossip, is
believed to be the person who started
the fight after Miss Einhorn scolded
her for messing up her long division.

I erased all of that and started over. This one showed my
frustration.

Maddie Evans sent herself to Mr.
Shelly's office after three days of
no gossip caused her to release an
explosion of words in Miss Einhorn's
fourth-period math class. Maddie, a
seventh grader known for her juicy
stories, claims a case of temporary
insanity caused her to loudly report
every piece of gossip she'd heard or
witnessed since Friday, when her best
friend cruelly made her stop gossiping.

Usually gossip was far more interesting than the truth.

Chapter Eight

"WHO'S THAT?"

The question came from Emma, who was sitting behind the girl across from me in social studies the next morning. We were all waiting for the results of midterms. I turned to follow Emma's stare. She was watching something out the window. By then only a few of us were looking out, but we were all looking at the same thing.

It was Miss Hollywood, surrounded by those same two guys who had been with her Saturday morning. They were heading down the sidewalk toward the parking lot. If Miss Golden was trying to keep all of this top secret, why was she walking out there in broad daylight, in front of everyone?

"Nobody knows," Liza Cross said. "She's been here all morning."

"I heard she's here to buy the school," Kimberly Browning said. "They're going to tear it down and build a shopping center."

That was the most ridiculous thing I'd ever heard. But it immediately spiraled out of control.

"Where will we go to school?" Liza asked.

Kimberly shrugged. "They'll probably combine us with Beechwood Middle."

Emma spoke up. "Ugh. They have roaches the size of cats in that school."

Did these people even listen to themselves? "They aren't selling the school," I said.

Everyone was looking at me. I was the one who knew things. I'd straighten all this out.

I looked out at Miss Hollywood and her helpers, climbing into a car. How much could I say?

"She's helping improve the school," I said. "She was asking me questions."

Wrong move. Of course, Kimberly latched right on to that. "About improving the school?"

"Like what?" Emma added.

"I'll bet they're going to remodel the whole place," Kimberly said. "Maybe we'll even get carpet."

"And TVs." This from Liza, who sounded even more excited.

"I doubt we'll get TVs in school," I corrected.

"Why not?" Kevin Jones asked. He was seated behind Emma. "It could be educational. They could show documentaries about the war or something."

When Liza spoke, she had a dreamy expression. "And they could set up a whole break area with big, soft sofas and a snack bar . . ."

"And cell phone rooms, so we could talk in private," Kevin said.

I bit my lip to keep from speaking up about what we'd discussed in Mr. Shelly's office yesterday about a break area. Miss Golden would be glad to know our idea was a hit with students, though. If only I could tell her.

Miss Turner showed up, passing our midterms out. My sixth B. I was betting Vi got all A's. For the rest of social studies, I worried about what I'd said. I'd just said Miss Golden wanted to improve the school. That was fact. Still, I worried what would happen next. If it spread through the school and got back to Vi, and she found out I was the one who had started it, I'd be in big trouble.

It wasn't a good sign that everyone seemed to latch on to me as we were leaving class. I looked around nervously as I stepped out into the hallway. No sign of Vi, but that didn't mean we wouldn't turn a corner and run directly into her.

"Did you meet her?"

"What did she say?"

"What does she plan to do?"

The questions were unending, which was a good thing, since I wasn't answering any of them. Everyone's words were jumbled so closely together, there wouldn't have been time for me to say anything even if I wanted to. I just kept walking, going faster as I headed toward my locker.

"I need to get stuff for my next class," I announced to no one in particular. That somehow helped me shake a couple of them, but Emma and Kimberly remained. And then, as I was turning my locker combination while wishing they'd all just vanish, I heard Jessica's voice.

"What's up?" she asked.

"You know that new woman who showed up at school today?" Kimberly asked. No, Jessica had no idea who they were talking about, I was pretty sure. But Kimberly continued anyway. "Maddie says she's here to completely remodel the whole school."

"I didn't say that," I said, whirling around to face all of them. "I said no such thing."

Only Jessica's eyes widened at that outburst. Everyone else just stared at me like they were waiting for me to say something else.

"You said she was here to redo the school," Emma pointed out. "I heard you."

"I'm lost," Jessica said.

"I met her in the principal's office." I sighed. "She's really nice. She was talking about some improvements, that's all I know. Now, I really need to get to class."

I wasn't sure if I'd said the wrong thing or not, but that was all I could think to do to fix it. My next step was to run.

Jessica and Sydney were waiting for me after last period. Usually Vi and I caught up with them outside, in the area where the buses were, so I knew what this was about.

"Spill it," Sydney said.

I clamped my lips together and shook my head. Most important, though, I kept walking.

"Come on, you know stuff," Jessica pleaded, rushing to keep up with me. "You have to tell us. We're your besties."

That tugged at me, but I couldn't say anything. Any second now we'd run into Vi and she'd overhear everything we were saying.

"I didn't say anything," I said. "I was just trying to make them feel better. They were all worried we would be merging with Beechwood Middle."

Sydney gasped. "They're sending us to Beechwood Middle?"

"No." This was just getting worse by the minute. I needed to stop talking. Maybe I should stay home for the rest of the thirty days.

"Then why did you say they were?" Sydney asked.

"I didn't say that. I was telling you what the other people in class were guessing, but it isn't true. I was correcting them on it."

I'd stopped walking and now was looking at both of them, trying to let them know that it was very important that they understand this. This wasn't my gossip. It was other people's gossip. It was starting to hit me, though, that Vi was blaming all of this gossip stuff on me when I wasn't the only one who gossiped. Sure, I did my part, but even when I wasn't trying to gossip, they were all filling in the blanks, making gossip out of things I didn't say.

"Vi!" Sydney called out. Vi. She was still speaking

to Sydney and Jess and . . . well . . . everyone else who was gossiping their little mouths off. The only person she wasn't speaking to was the one person who had stopped gossiping.

I had to stop this. Whether Vi was speaking to me or not, I had to tell her what was going on before she heard it from someone else.

"We have to talk," I said to Vi. "Something's happened."

"Vi! I've been looking for you."

Vi was still looking at me when Kathina Freeman pulled her attention away. Kathina was running up beside me, but her attention was focused on Vi. I held in a groan. If Kathina was talking to us, it had to be about Travis, and if it was about Travis, I might be in even more trouble. I hadn't said anything to anyone about it since I'd promised not to gossip, but that didn't mean I couldn't still get into trouble somehow, as I was finding out.

"Guess who was asking about you?" Kathina said. She had one of those looks on her face that I knew all too well. It was a look that said she knew something nobody else knew and she couldn't wait to tell someone.

I missed that feeling.

"Who?" Vi asked. Her level of excitement didn't even come close to Kathina's. In fact, Vi sounded kind of bored.

"Travis Fisher," Kathina answered. Her smile had widened so much, I thought it might fall off her face. "He asked me how well I knew you."

I looked over at Vi. She had a puzzled look on her face. I wouldn't have expected her to frown over news like this.

"Exactly what did he say?" Vi asked.

"He asked how well I knew that Vivienne Lakewood girl," Kathina said. "I told him we go all the way back to first grade. He wanted to know what you were like."

This time I was the one to ask, "What did you say?"

This should be interesting, since Kathina and Vi *didn't* go all the way back to first grade. Sure, we'd all gone to school together, but Kathina and Vi had maybe had four conversations in all that time. One of those conversations was the one where Vi had found out I told Travis she liked him.

"I said you were really sweet," Kathina told her. "Kind of quiet, but very classy. Like an old-timey movie star. I think he might like you. Whoops, that's my ride. See ya."

We'd stepped through the school entrance onto the overcrowded walkway in front of the school. In front of us, kids were climbing into the school buses lined up, ready to leave in just a few minutes. Instead of heading toward our bus, though, Vi stopped to stare after Kathina.

"What did she mean by that?" Vi asked.

Vi was speaking to me. Well, she'd said the words to the air in front of her, so it sounded almost like she was talking to herself, but if there was a small chance she might speak to me, I had to go with it.

"Let's get on the bus and talk about it," I rushed to say before she could realize she was kind-of-sort-of talking to me. We had more to talk about than Kathina. I wanted to warn her about everything that had happened at school that day.

"Old-timey movie star?" Vi asked, unfazed by me trying to urge her toward the bus. "What does that mean? That makes me sound boring."

"No, it doesn't. You're classy. Like Audrey Hepburn or Julia Roberts. You know, an old-timey movie star."

That didn't seem to help. She still wasn't moving.

"And she said I was quiet," Vi said. "I'm not quiet. I'm very talkative. He's going to think I'm one of those people who never talk."

"I don't think he'll think that, but we're going to miss our bus."

I started walking and, thank goodness, Vi followed. I guess it was either that or stand there talking to herself. She was still trying to put it all together as we walked, though.

"I don't think I'm old-timey," Vi was saying. "I do all

this interior design stuff. Why couldn't she talk about that?"

"She probably doesn't know," I replied. "Did you hear the part where she said he might like you?"

That was the important part, I figured. It was huge news, but she couldn't see past worrying about the other stuff. To me, that seemed more negative than all my gossip, but who was I to say?

Besides, if Travis liked her, that meant telling him hadn't been such a bad thing. And since I was on the verge of being busted for starting rumors, any help I could have would be good.

"Come over?" Vi asked. I could tell from the pleading look in her eyes she wasn't just asking. She didn't want to be alone. I could see that. I didn't want to be alone at my house, either.

There was no way I'd say no. I missed my best friend. I didn't even realize how much until she spoke to me again. I felt this giant wave of relief wash over me as we both got onto the bus and started toward Vi's house.

I didn't even have to call my mom to tell her I was going over to Vi's. We'd had so many days of hanging out at each other's houses that both of our moms knew if we weren't home, we were at the other person's house. That was just how it worked.

But the weird thing here was, I hadn't been to Vi's house since our initial blowup. At first I wasn't sure if I'd be invited over until the thirty days were up. So it was a relief to be camped out on Vi's couch with baked veggie potato chips and coconut water. That was the closest thing to junk food we could find at her house. My house wouldn't have been much better.

"I have to show him I'm outgoing," Vi said. "I don't want him to think I'm shy."

"Why don't you just talk to him?" I asked. "I could introduce you."

It beat offering to talk to him *for* her, which I was sure would just make things worse between us. I should have known that wouldn't work for Vi, though. She was terrified to talk to boys. Especially boys she liked as much as she liked Travis Fisher.

"That's what an outgoing girl would do," I reminded her. "Shy girls are afraid to talk to boys."

"I don't want him to think I'm chasing him," Vi said worriedly. "I just want to get to know him without all that."

I wasn't sure how to help her there. Maybe she just wanted someone to listen to her. So that was what I did. I quietly munched on chips while Vi talked.

"Maybe if he knew my interests . . . ," Vi said. "He'd like me then, right?"

I nodded but she didn't even look at me. She just kept talking.

"I could show him what I'm doing with my room," Vi commented. "But he probably wouldn't care about that, would he?"

I thought for a second. There was no natural way to let him know about Vi's decorating talent. He probably wouldn't care about what she was doing to her bedroom anyway. That was more of a girl thing. What we needed was a way for him to see her talent in person.

"We need a school project," Vi said. "Some way we could work together on something."

She was having the same thought I was. But I had one thing she didn't—knowledge that Troy Middle School may very well have a project they could work on together. Only I couldn't tell her about it.

"Maybe if people knew about your stuff," I said, pointing to her sketch pad on the table between us. "We should make sure the people in charge know."

Vi looked at me. At least she noticed I was there. I was beginning to wonder.

"People in charge," she added.

People like Miss Golden and her two guys. People who could put Vi to work showing off her talents to Travis Fisher and the world.

"Mr. Shelly, for one," I said instead. Because the whole Miss Golden thing would have been impossible to explain without gossiping. "And maybe some of the teachers."

"I already showed Miss Hunter," Vi pointed out. "Why would I tell anyone else about it?"

That wasn't so easy to answer. I took a shot at it anyway.

"If other teachers know about your talents, Travis will know about it," I said. "Understand?"

She thought about it for a second before saying, "Nah. I don't think so. It's no big deal, anyway. I'm sure Travis and I have something in common and it probably has nothing to do with decorating bedrooms."

But if she didn't tell Mr. Shelly about her skills, the crew from *24-Hour Makeover* might not find out about them. They might come in, start doing their renovations, and never involve Vi. It would be all my fault because I knew about it and didn't tell her. She'd never, ever forgive me for not telling me her favorite show was coming to our school. But I *couldn't* tell Vi.

"So what's going on with you?" Vi asked suddenly.

I looked up, alarmed. Was she on to me? Did she know

all about the gossip that had been going around the school? I'd have to explain myself and I had no explanation. I hadn't even prepared for this moment—

"The no-gossiping thing." Vi's voice cut into my thoughts. "How's that going for you?"

I was surprised she asked that. We hadn't talked for so long that now that we'd started, things felt touchy between us. But since she'd brought it up, I had to give her an answer.

"It's not easy," I said. "People keep assuming things and reading into things that I'm saying."

That was my way of preparing her for hearing that I'd started some massive rumor at school. This way hopefully she wouldn't get as mad if she heard something like that. But she was looking at me with her head tilted to the side a little.

"What do you mean?" she asked, curious.

"They expect me to gossip, so even when I don't say anything, they assume that's saying something," I told her.

She thought about that a second. "I see."

"Like today," I said. "There was this strange woman walking across the front lawn of school. Everyone asked who it was and started making up all these crazy stories. I told the truth about her—"

"Which *was*?" Vi asked.

I clamped my mouth shut and stared. Oh no. I wasn't going to walk into that trap.

"Oh, I get it," Vi answered for me. "Like right now I assume the truth is some huge thing you can't tell me, so I'm making stuff up in my head?"

I nodded. She continued.

"And then that person tells someone else and says you're the one who said it," she added.

"Exactly." I sighed in relief. It felt like I was letting out a breath I'd been holding in for the past few days. "Even if I state a fact, they add all kinds of things to it."

"Hmmm. Let me think about that. That might count."

"What? How can that count? I can't spend the next twenty-six days hiding in a hole somewhere."

"The whole thing was, you aren't supposed to gossip," Vi said, handing the chip bag to me and standing up. "Look up the definition of gossip. It's not just what you say but what you hear, too."

"I'm pretty sure gossiping is just spreading gossip," I told her.

"But if you're listening and nodding along while someone is gossiping, you're making it worse. It was thirty days of no gossip."

"Thirty days of not talking about other people or writing the *Troy Tattler*," I said, standing to face off with her. "That's what you said."

"But as you can see, you're spreading gossip without even talking," she said. "If I hear someone gossiping, I remove myself from the situation immediately. If they ask my opinion, I tell them I prefer only to say nice things about people."

"You've listened to us gossip for as long as I can remember," I pointed out. "I think you were listening to gossip when we were in preschool."

"I don't listen," she said. "Most of the time, I really tune all of you out when you're talking about other people."

I crossed my arms over my chest, surprised. Seriously? She was trying to make me believe while she was sitting next to me, doodling on her sketch pad or doing her math homework, she wasn't halfway listening?

"I know you too well to believe that," I said. "I've known you all my life."

Vi's expression softened at the reminder that we'd been friends so long. I half hoped she'd suddenly realize how silly this was and everything could go back to being normal. *More* than halfway.

"It's never been about the actual gossip," Vi said. "That's what I want you to see."

I gave her a quizzical look and waited for her to say more. If it wasn't about gossip, what *was* it about?

"Never mind." Vi waved a hand in the air dismissively. "Just do whatever you want."

"I'm trying," I argued. "Can't I get some credit for that? I'm doing everything I can do to make you happy, and I just don't know what else to do."

"I want you to make yourself happy," Vi said. "But until you figure out that this isn't about gossip but about our friendship and how I *trusted* you to keep my secret, I can't help you. Maybe you'll never figure it out. Maybe it's just a lost cause."

"What does that mean?" I asked as Vi grabbed our trash and started toward the kitchen.

"If our friendship is really important to you, you'll figure it out yourself," Vi called back as she disappeared through the doorway.

Chapter Nine

I SAW MISS GOLDEN AGAIN FIRST THING THE NEXT morning. Okay, so I actually kind of chased her down, following her from her car in the visitors' lot to the teachers' lounge, where I saw her standing outside, waiting for someone to let her in.

"Maddie Evans!"

I was so surprised that she remembered both my first and last names, I skidded to a stop several feet away from her. Maybe I'd told her Monday in Mr. Shelly's office, but someone like Miss Golden was so busy, I wouldn't expect her to remember something like my name.

"Hi, Miss Golden," I said.

"Please," she waved away my words. "Call me Ashley. 'Miss Golden' makes me feel old."

"Okay," I said. Although I doubted I'd ever be comfortable calling her by her first name. "Are you here to see one of the teachers?"

I knew I was being nosy, but I didn't think it was against the rules to be nosy. Just to tell other people what I heard.

"I thought I'd pop my head in," she answered. "Is anyone in there?"

I looked at the closed door. I didn't know anything about what went on behind that door. The teachers' lounge was top secret in this school.

"You know what?" Miss Golden said suddenly. "Never mind. I'd rather walk with you. Why don't you show me around?"

That threw me off for a moment. She'd walk around school with me? Being seen with her was sure to make people ask me questions later. Questions like, *Who was that woman? What was she doing here?* Questions I couldn't answer without starting rumors.

But what else could I say? I couldn't pass up an opportunity like this. I started toward the gym, where all the torture happened. Luckily, there weren't enough people around yet that it made a scene. Miss Golden probably knew that.

"What's this hallway?" she asked as we passed the language arts area. That was one of the worst hallways, with some kind of strange stuffing hanging from the ceiling and a couple of the tiles missing altogether. The floors were a weird yellowish shade that looked like paper after it had been around a long, long time.

But instead of avoiding it, Miss Golden took a sharp left turn into the Hallway of Yuck. She was squinting up at the ceiling, reminding me why she was here. Miss Golden saw this as a great opportunity, while most of us looked at it as hopeless.

"Do you have classes down here?" Miss Golden asked.

I nodded, pointing at my second-period classroom. To be honest, I never paid much attention to this hallway after my first couple of days of school. It was just something I went through to get to class.

"This is uninhabitable," Miss Golden said, looking around. Her mouth was hanging open and her eyes were wide. "Kids can't learn in a place like this."

I might not know what "uninhabitable" meant, but I knew that last part. I figured it was a good sign. I mean, if she'd walked around the school and found it perfect, she wouldn't want to bring her cameras in, right?

But it wouldn't do any good to bring those cameras in

if Vi wasn't a part of it. So I had to do it. I had to give it a try, right?

"We have some students that are really good at this stuff," I said, my heart starting to beat like crazy. "My best friend, Vi, is redoing her own room, paint and everything."

Miss Golden didn't stop and beg to know everything about Vi as I'd hoped. She just kept looking around.

"Paint is the least of the problems," she said. "With something like this, you have to redo the whole ceiling. Look at those tiles. And brick walls? Those need to be covered with drywall."

I didn't know what drywall was, but Vi would.

"Vi would love to learn about stuff like that," I suggested. I didn't know if it would count in Vi's rules, but I saw it as my one chance to help Vi out. "I'll bet she and a few of us other students could redo this whole hallway if the school would let us. We could make it a weekend project. Do you think they'd go for that?"

I gave Miss Golden a hopeful look. She looked at me as if seeing me for the first time. I'd gone too far. She was on to me. Now she'd cut me off and not speak to me again, with no chance at all of Vi being involved in rebuilding. They'd have every kid in school help *but* me and Vi.

"That shows initiative," Miss Golden said. "I like that. I'll see if I can talk Mr. Shelly into it."

I nodded, trying not to look too excited. If I looked excited, she'd figure out what I was up to. Nobody got excited about hanging drywall, did they?

"Now, show me your break area," Miss Golden requested. She started walking, peeking into empty class-rooms as she went.

"Break area?" I asked, rushing to keep up with her. "You mean the room where the vending machines are?"

She slowed and turned to look at me. At least that gave me a chance to catch up.

"There's no break area?" she asked.

"The cafeteria?"

"No, somewhere you can hang out during your breaks."

"We don't have a room like that," I said. "Just a vending machine that gives juice and bottled water."

Had this woman never been in a middle school before? I realized as she took off toward the cafeteria that she prob-ably hadn't. She was used to going to hospitals and churches and stuff. She probably thought that with this many people, a middle school was sure to have a lounge . . . and the teachers' lounge didn't count.

"Well, that's wrong," she said. "You need a place you can call your own."

"They give us lockers," I offered, thinking of the way we all gathered around each other's lockers between classes. Vi's locker was one of my favorite hangouts. I'd probably spent more time there than at my own.

"That's just a place to store things," Miss Golden said. "You need a comfortable place. I see fun chairs with butterfly designs. Maybe even built-in power plugs to charge cell phones."

The funny thing was, she was standing in the middle of the cafeteria as she said it. The big, empty, sterile cafeteria, where the only background noise was the sound of workers getting lunch ready. This room couldn't be further from what she was describing.

"I doubt the school would go for that," I told her. I had no idea who made those decisions, but I knew they were more focused on helping us learn than making sure our phones had a full charge. Miss Golden wasn't thinking like that, though. She was thinking in terms of what would work best for her TV show.

Maybe she wasn't so wrong about that. Really. The

school wanted to look good on TV, so they'd be more likely to go along with what Miss Golden said. She might be able to talk them into it.

"And this cafeteria needs work." Sighing, Miss Golden turned to look at me. She seemed to suddenly remember I was with her. I saw her slightly panicked look as she tried to remember if she'd given anything away. "Why don't you show me to your first class?"

Showing Miss Golden my first-period class was what did it. By then the school was filled with students, rushing to get to class before the bell rang, so plenty of people saw me leading Miss Golden down the hallway. Those people included Jessica and Sydney, who gave me a curious look, and Kimberly Browning and Chelsea Tucker, who were in my first class.

"Okay, let's hear it," Kimberly said. "That's the woman who's here to fix the school, right?"

What was it Vi wanted me to learn? Not to break people's trust? Miss Golden hadn't actually said this was supposed to be secret, but someone didn't have to say that something was a secret for it to be one.

Plus, speaking about it was gossiping, and not only was that breaking my promise to Vi, it might risk our chances at being on *24-Hour Makeover*. It wasn't guaranteed yet, I assumed.

"I don't know," I said with a shrug. "She wanted me to show her around."

And that was the truth. So what if I'd searched the Internet and learned a few things about her? It was still not 100 percent true unless she'd told me herself.

"You have to know something," Chelsea accused.

I felt that little tug that had led me to start gossiping in the first place. Back when I was Fatty Maddie, Chelsea and all her friends were the pretty ones, looking down on me. I wanted so badly to be part of their little group, but no matter what I said, they didn't like me.

Then one day I found out Sarah Dooley's dad had left. I heard one of the neighbors talking to Mom about it, which made sense since Sarah lived in my neighborhood back then. I didn't mean to tell everyone, but I was sitting with Chelsea and Kathina during recess and they were asking why Sarah was out, so I told them.

That was when I learned that knowing things and telling them made people like you.

Well, they only liked me for a day or so, until they got more answers from Sarah than they could from me. But it was enough to show me what could happen if I said something people wanted to hear. So from then on, I tried to find information and share it with others.

Now here we were. Full circle. Sitting in first period, with Chelsea wanting to know what I knew. It wasn't that I thought she'd like me if I told her. She'd make fun of me with her friends, and next thing I knew, I'd be Fatty Maddie again. She pretty much had no opinion of me other than the fact that I knew things. It was just that I was afraid if I didn't answer her questions, she'd stop liking me.

"I think she knows something," Kimberly said to Chelsea. "You notice she's not denying it."

"Seriously," I insisted. "She hasn't told me who she is. She just asked some questions about the language arts wing."

"She wants to redo the language arts wing," Kimberly enthused. She looked over at Chelsea. "You don't think—?"

"I do," Chelsea said. They both turned to look at me, and Chelsea said, "She's here from one of those makeover TV shows, isn't she? They wouldn't just make over the school for no reason."

"They wouldn't make over the school for a TV show, either," I added. "That's silly."

I felt a little panic growing deep in the pit of my belly. They'd figured it out. They'd guessed it. Now all that would have to happen was that they'd tell some people, it would be all over the school, and I'd be the one blamed for it. I had to throw them off the scent somehow.

"She works for the school board," I lied. It might be starting a rumor, but was it gossip if I was trying to fix a problem?

"You just said you didn't know who she was," Chelsea reminded me with a frown. She gave me a challenging look. "I think you're making stuff up now."

"Why would I make it up? She works for the school board. I'd make up something more exciting than that if I were making up things."

I paused to let that one sink in. Thank goodness it seemed to work. Chelsea still looked like she wasn't sure, but Kimberly was nodding. She bought it.

"It *is* a bad story," Kimberly agreed. "Like telling someone you spent the weekend cleaning your room."

"I guess," Chelsea said. "I don't know why the school board would be looking at the school, though."

"Have you looked around?" Kimberly asked. "This place is falling apart."

I turned around in my seat and faced the front of the room. If I waited for class to start, they couldn't talk about this with me anymore. As the final bell rang, I felt a tap on my shoulder and turned to find Chelsea leaning in.

"You can tell me," she whispered. "I won't tell anyone."

She sat back in her seat as class started, leaving me to think about what she'd said. It would be nice to tell someone what I knew. Just one person I could confide in. I wanted to tell Vi, but she was the one person I couldn't tell. If I told Jessica or Sydney, they'd tell Vi, so that wasn't an option either. It had to be someone who never talked to Vi. Someone who probably didn't even know Vi's name. Chelsea would be perfect.

Plus, if I told Chelsea, she'd be impressed that the producer for a TV show had asked me to show her around the school, for sure. And because I knew about *24-Hour Makeover* before anyone else, they'd think I was smarter than most of the other kids around here.

I'd tell her, just not yet. I'd wait until gym, our next class together, and tell her everything that had happened.

Chapter Ten

The Troy Tattler

By Maddie Evans

Who is the woman seen wandering the halls of Troy Middle School with our very own Madison Evans? Rumor has it she is the producer for a major TV show. If a TV producer is spending this much time at our school, that can mean only one thing.

Troy Middle School, get ready for your makeover.

Since I already got in trouble for playing with my phone in class, I was writing the *Troy Tattler* in my head. It couldn't be written, published, and handed out, so that was good enough anyway. Maybe if I wrote it here, I wouldn't tell Chelsea about it when we had our second class together in fifteen minutes. I could just get it out of my system now.

The bell rang. Time to go.

I stood slowly, clutching my books in front of me protectively. I wasn't ready yet. I wouldn't tell her. I wouldn't tell anyone anything. I'd decided that by the time I reached the door, and with every step, I was surer of it. If I had this many bad thoughts about it, it couldn't be right.

I held my head high, telling myself that nobody else could bully me into gossiping. Nobody could make me say anything I didn't want to say. I was in charge here, and if they didn't like me, tough.

For a second—a very brief, fleeting second—I thought I might have a glimpse of what Vi was trying to get me to see.

But before I could dwell on that long, Jessica called out to me. "Maddie, over here."

That was odd. Jessica, Sydney, and Sarah were all lined up in front of Jessica's locker. They were staring at me expectantly, but Sydney wasn't smiling. She looked like she was expecting me to say I didn't know anything.

"Chelsea says you know something," Sydney said as

I drew closer. She didn't keep her voice down, and both Sarah and Jessica gave her a look.

"You have to tell us," Jessica said. "Are we going to be on *24-Hour Makeover*?"

My jaw dropped. How on earth had they figured that out?

"I—I don't know," I stammered. "Where did you hear that?"

"Everyone was talking about it in second period," Sarah answered. "They said you know all about it."

I was doomed. I felt a little sick. This was far bigger than Vi finding out and being mad at me. This could ruin our school's chances. If it was supposed to be top secret and I was responsible for it getting out, I could mess it up for everyone.

"That's the silliest thing I've ever heard," I said, stepping away from them. I'd just turn and head off to my locker and that would be that. They'd tell people. . . .

What?

That it was true? That I'd run off, so I had to be hiding something?

I froze. Nothing I could do would make this any better. But there had to be something I could say that would change it all. I thought for a second, looking at each of the three friends in front of me. The truth. It was all I could do at this point.

"If it gets out, it might not happen," I warned. "It's supposed to be secret."

"So it's true?" Jessica said, her eyes lit up with excitement. "That's awesome."

"But you can't tell anyone," I said. "Seriously. It has to be kept under wraps until it's announced."

"We can do that." Jessica looked at Sarah and Sydney. "Right?"

"Right," Sarah said.

Sydney narrowed her eyes at me. "Why do you know and nobody else does?"

"I don't know," I said. More truth. "I just know she's been hanging around here a lot lately and I looked her up online. It could be completely wrong. She could be another Ashley Golden—"

I stopped myself from saying more as I realized I could be saying way too much. Giving them her name and all. They'd of course search for her online and find out everything I'd discovered. Then they'd start their own rumors. I couldn't be blamed for that, though, could I?

"We'll keep it secret," Jessica promised. "Come on."

"I'll walk with Maddie," Sarah offered, sliding out from in between the two girls. Sydney still didn't believe anything I said and I wasn't sure why. She'd always questioned me a little more than anyone else, but this was worse than ever.

It still was bugging me as Sarah and I started walking. It would bother me the rest of the day, along with everything else. What was bugging me most of all, though, was what Vi had said. It was still with me. Was I really all that concerned about what other people thought about me?

"I wanted to talk to you about Aiden Lewis." Sarah's voice pulled me out of my thoughts. "You told people he likes me."

"He used to," I said with a shrug. "It was kind of common knowledge."

Warning bells were going off in my head. Just because the entire school thought I'd spread the rumor about *24-Hour Makeover* didn't mean I had a free pass to break my promise to Vi. I thought about what she'd said. Saying bad things about people was bad? But what if it was something good? What if I was helping Sarah by doing this?

I spotted Aiden up ahead, rushing toward class, and got an idea. "Come with me," I told Sarah.

"Where are you going?" Sarah called after me as I rushed toward Aiden. I could feel her falling behind, which probably meant she didn't want me to do this, but this was the only alternative to gossiping. It was all I could think to do.

"Aiden!" I called out as I drew closer. He slowed to a stop and turned to face me. "I want you to meet someone."

I turned, but Sarah had stopped. She was looking around like she was thinking about running in the other direction. Who would have thought Sarah Dooley would be shy? She was the first person in our class to get a real boyfriend, so I would have thought she had more courage than any of us.

"Sarah, this is Aiden. Aiden, Sarah."

Yes, I introduced them anyway. If they were going to stand there like that, someone had to do something. They nodded at each other, which was weird since you probably could have lined up three cars between them.

"Great. Now you know each other. I'm going to class."

No gossip. No rumors. They now knew each other, so there was no excuse for them to do all this talking back and forth.

Still, as I headed toward the gym, I couldn't help but worry that I'd made Sarah mad. If I'd just told her about Aiden liking her, she might have been happier. It made no sense. Wasn't meeting a boy you might like better than talking about it to all your friends for months and never getting to even talk to him? Maybe that was just me.

I thought back to Vi. *This* was exactly what she'd been talking about, wasn't it? My footsteps slowed and

I turned around to look back at Sarah and Aiden. They were standing there, talking to each other, looking very uncomfortable.

I was always interfering in people's lives. Why? Why couldn't I just let people do things for themselves? Was Vi right about me?

Realizing I was standing there staring at the two of them, I turned and headed toward the gym. Whether my heart was in the right place didn't matter. That was what Vi tried to tell me. I think I was finally getting it, but could I change? *That* was the real question.

Chelsea was waiting for me in the locker room.

Not *waiting*, exactly. She was standing in front of one of the lockers, changing into her shorts and T-shirt, but the second I walked in, she stopped everything and looked at me.

"Here she is," Chelsea said loudly. Everyone turned to look at me. An entire row of girls I played volleyball and basketball and soccer with every day in this class. Most of the time they paid no attention to me at all, but today I was the star.

"Chelsea said you know that TV producer," Wynona Jennings said. "How do we get on the show?"

"Look." I held up my hand to stop any more questions. Then I saw them all looking at me and froze.

This was where I was supposed to tell them this had all gotten way, *way* out of hand. I'd say that I knew nothing about any TV show and that they should just wait until they heard something and stop talking about things they knew nothing about. I could even imitate Vi's mature way of saying things like that.

But what would probably happen? I could see it now. I'd give my little speech and everyone's expressions would harden. They'd turn back to their lockers and not speak to me as we all got dressed with tension in the air between us. They'd then head out to the gym floor, leaving me in here all alone. By the time I joined them, nobody would be speaking to me. Nobody would speak to me ever again.

"It's supposed to be top secret," I said.

"We won't tell anyone," Chelsea said. They all moved in closer. Lockers clicked closed and everything in the locker room got very, very quiet.

And this is what made it so hard to stop gossiping. That was the best feeling ever. Everyone was hanging on my every word, anxious to hear what I'd say next. They couldn't wait to hear it. I was important. People *liked* me.

"Okay." I lowered my voice to barely above a whisper.

"Her name is Ashley Golden and she's a producer for *24-Hour Makeover*. She's here to do a show on the school. I showed her around and she asked about the language arts wing and the cafeteria. She wants to create a break area for us."

"A break area?" Amie Mondale asked. "Like, with TV screens and video games?"

"No, silly." Chelsea shot a glare in her direction. "A place with vending machines and seats, I'm sure."

"And somewhere to talk on our cell phones if we have to call our parents," I said. "Maybe even with chargers so we can keep our batteries going all day."

"That would be so cool," Dawes Adams said, her eyes wide. "I wonder if they'd let us bring our laptops in."

"I'm sure they would, as long as we only used them on break," Wynona added. "Plus, there will be chargers, so it's perfect."

As they all started discussing all the things they could do with their laptops during our fifteen-minute break, I was having major second thoughts. I changed into my shorts and headed out to the gym, letting them talk it out. It wasn't like telling them had suddenly made me the most popular person ever. It had just given them all something to talk about without me.

Now that I thought about it, this was how it had always been. I handed out gossip while everyone stared at me, eating up every word I said. As long as the information kept coming, I was the gossip queen. But the second I ran out of information, people went on to something else and I was no more interesting than anyone else in school.

I sat down on the front row of bleachers and looked out across the empty gym. Had I just totally destroyed my friendship with Vi for thirty seconds of popularity?

Chapter Eleven

EVERYTHING WAS OKAY. FOR NOW, AT LEAST. VI seemed to have no idea what was going on, and Jessica and Sydney weren't talking about it, just as I'd requested.

"Vi and I are going shopping Saturday," Sarah told me when I sat down at our table at lunch. "We're picking out curtains."

"Can I come?" I asked. I looked from Vi to Sarah. Not that I was all that excited to spend all day looking at curtains, but it would make Vi happy. Besides, by then she'd be supermad at me, so maybe if we had plans to go look at curtains, she'd have to forgive me. It was worth a try, anyway.

"You want to?" Sarah threw out, looking down at her food.

"I can't think of anything I'd rather do," I said, giving Vi a meaningful look. I meant it, too. Now that I knew I might be in my final minutes of being Vi's BFF, even picking out curtains with her would be nice.

I suddenly thought back to a time when I was crying on the playground in first grade. We'd all been working on an art project and I was put on a team with Chelsea, her neighbor Erica, and a girl named Mary Jo Myers. We were all supposed to work together, but the three of them cut me out completely, acting like I wasn't even there. If I spoke, they ignored me. If I tried to do something, they pulled it out of my reach. I was in tears by the time we broke for recess, sure nobody in the world liked me.

But Vi hung out with me. She told me that those girls were mean and she didn't know why I wanted to be friends with them anyway. She was right, I realized back then. I had Vi as a best friend, so why did I need anyone else? For the rest of the day and a few weeks afterward, I tried to focus on the people I liked who liked me back and to forget about those mean girls, but it was only a matter of time before I was once again trying to get them to like me.

That was how I felt right now, sitting next to Vi, with Jessica and Sydney across from us. We even had a new friend Sarah, who was gushing about how I'd introduced her to Aiden and she really thought she might like him and wasn't I the awesomest person ever? I didn't want to talk about some reality TV show. I wanted to hear what Vi had to say about her redecorating project.

I sat up straight, my eyes widening, as I realized I really did want to listen to Vi's decorating plans. What was happening to me? Was this no-gossip project making permanent changes to my personality?

"Are you sure we won't have something else to do this weekend?" Jessica asked. "I mean, you know . . ."

I flashed her a warning look, as did Sarah. We didn't know when *24-Hour Makeover* was taping, but that wasn't why I was glaring. Vi was looking down at her tray, but Jessica's words brought her head back up again.

"Like what?" Vi asked. She didn't sound too concerned, so maybe we could just blow it off.

"Nothing," I said. "Jess was just thinking we might want to come hang out at her house, but we can do that anytime."

"No way." Vi shook her head. "Maddie is mine this weekend. She promised to help me with this. My mom's out of town Saturday, so it's my chance to do whatever I want. Otherwise, she'll be standing over me, talking me into some kind of ruffly, checkered thing."

"Yikes," I said, mostly to keep Jessica from speaking up.

But Jessica's attention was on something just past my right shoulder.

"Red alert," she said.

Not that I could have done anything about it, but by the time I turned around, Chelsea was already right behind me. She slid onto the seat next to me. Kathina moved around to sit next to Sydney.

"So . . . let's talk about the show," Chelsea said.

"You still haven't told us how we get on it," Kathina said. "We want to be on camera."

I was all too aware of Vi, sitting next to me and watching every bit of this. She didn't say anything, but she didn't have to. I knew that if I looked at her, she'd have a big question mark on her expression.

"We aren't supposed to talk about it until it's announced," Jessica whispered. "It's top secret."

Chelsea rolled her eyes. "By the time it's announced, it'll be too late. We need to know how to be first in line when *24-Hour Makeover* comes here to shoot their show."

"What are they talking about, Maddie?" Vi asked. "Is *24-Hour Makeover* really coming here?"

I looked at her, not sure what to say. If I denied knowing anything about it, everyone around me would correct me. If I told her it was all just a rumor and we weren't 100 percent sure about it, I'd be busted for gossiping for sure. Even if I said it was definite, it was pretty obvious here that I was the one who'd started everyone talking about it. They were coming to me for answers.

"Maddie met the producer," Kathina explained. "Hey, maybe there's a way we could get Travis Fisher to be on the same team as us."

That wasn't helping. It was as if Kathina's mention of Travis's name reminded Vi of what had gotten me into trouble with her in the first place. And now, here we were, in the middle of the biggest gossip session I'd been involved in for as long as I could remember. I wanted out.

"May I speak with you a moment?" I asked Vi. I figured it was better if we did this alone.

Vi wasn't looking at me, though. Her attention was fully focused on Kathina.

"So you're telling me that Maddie found out about this *24-Hour Makeover* thing," Vi said slowly.

"Yes," Kathina answered.

"And she told everyone it was happening," Vi said.

"Yes." This from both Kathina *and* Chelsea.

"And now everyone's talking about it," Vi finished.

"They're supposed to be keeping it quiet," Sarah said. "Talking about it could blow it for us all."

Vi looked over at me. That settled it, I knew. Not only had I been starting gossip, I'd told people something I wasn't supposed to. That was gossiping of the worst kind.

"If you'll excuse me, I need to go to the girls' room before class." Vi stood, picked up her tray and her books, and left.

"I have to go," I said. I had to at least try. I didn't really stand a chance, but she was my best friend. Even if she didn't forgive me today, maybe she'd get over it eventually and forgive me.

"Wait!" I heard Chelsea call out as I took off after Vi. I just ignored her. There was nothing Chelsea could say that was more important than what I had to do now. I ignored the fact that everyone in the cafeteria was probably staring at me and ran until I was out in the hallway. Vi was only a few steps away.

When I spoke, I echoed Chelsea. "Wait. Vi."

She didn't wait. I should have expected that. I'd just have to catch up with her.

As I walked alongside her, she kept her gaze focused forward, not even glancing my way. This was it. She'd completely ignore me. That was fine. I just had to say what I needed to say and hope it got through to her.

"I know I messed up," I said. "I know I did. I know what you're trying to tell me and I'm working on it."

Still nothing. I had to keep talking anyway.

"Everyone was asking me," I defended myself. "They were all waiting for me to say something. I felt like if I didn't say something, they wouldn't like me anymore. When they're all staring at you, you feel the pressure. It's so hard. It's like a bad habit that I can't get rid of."

It wasn't the best speech I'd ever given, but it was all I could come up with at the last minute like this. I knew I had to think quickly, because pretty soon the bell would ring and she'd go to class and I'd have to give up. So I did my best.

"Doesn't it count that I'm trying?" I asked. My voice sounded kind of high-pitched, like I was begging. "I'm trying because you're my best friend and I want it to stay that way. Our friendship means that much to me. Doesn't that count for something?"

Nothing. Nothing but silence. Was I wasting my energy? I had to keep going.

"No matter what, you're always going to be my best friend," I said. "That won't change. I'll prove to you I've changed somehow."

Vi stopped and turned to look at me. There were tears in her eyes. That was the worst part of all. I could take it if she yelled and screamed at me, but this look of disappointment made my heart hurt.

"I just don't think I ever really knew you at all," Vi said. She took a deep breath and blinked rapidly until the tears seemed to go back where they'd come from. I knew she didn't want me to see her crying and would probably do everything she could to keep it all inside until I was gone. "I think what hurt most of all was that you didn't tell me. You told everyone but me."

I tilted my head slightly. "Tell you?"

"You know I'm into decorating. How could you keep something like this a secret from me, your best friend?"

"But—"

"You weren't supposed to gossip." She pressed her books to her chest and stepped stiffly back from me. "But you did. If you were going to tell the whole school and break your promise, you could have at least told me."

"You weren't speaking to me at first," I pointed out. "And once you were, I was afraid you'd get mad that I was gossiping."

"It's always this way," Vi said. The tears that had pooled in her eyes now spilled over onto her cheeks. "You talk to Sydney and Jess and share all these secrets and completely leave me out. I'm your best friend. I'm the one you're supposed to tell those things to."

I opened my mouth to respond, but nothing came out.

She was really upset. One thing was clear to me: She'd been upset about this for a long, *long* time and it was coming out now. How many signs had I missed? How long had Vi felt left out of our conversations?

Vi obviously took my silence as a sign that I had nothing to say. Shaking her head, she stepped away from me, finally turning to continue down the hall in the same direction we'd been walking, her head low and her shoulders slumped. That was it. I'd completely blown it. There was nothing I could do.

Chapter Twelve

The Troy Tattler

By Maddie Evans

We'll just call her the queen of ice. Everyone's noticed how Vi Lakewood has stopped speaking to her BFF, Maddie Evans, this week. Rumor has it she has a very good reason for giving Maddie the cold shoulder, though. Maddie knew something that was very important, and she didn't share it with Vi. Both Vi and Maddie are devastated at the loss of their lifelong friendship, but no matter what Maddie does, Vi won't break her silence. Can this friendship be saved?

One good thing came out of Vi getting mad at me over all this. I was free to gossip. And I hated every minute of it. Every time someone called me to talk about the show, I wanted to throw up. It just reminded me that Vi was no longer my friend. Unfortunately, Jess was calling me every fifteen minutes to talk about it.

"What are you going to wear?" Jessica asked. We'd just hung up about three minutes before that, and I was settling down onto my bed with my social studies textbook.

"When?" I asked, even though I knew what she was asking about. I was just so tired of talking about *24-Hour Makeover*, I'd welcome a discussion about anything at this point. Even the square footage of Vi's bedroom in direct proportion to the square footage of her brother's room.

"For *24-Hour Makeover*, silly," Jessica said. "It's only going to be national TV, so whatever you wear will be famous. That's so cool, when you think about it. I hear they're shooting this weekend."

The mention of this weekend reminded me that Vi and I were supposed to work on her room. We had planned to go shopping to pick out bedspreads and curtains. I wondered if she'd still do that without me. Maybe she'd get Syd to go with her and Sarah. The thought of that was like a stab to my heart.

"We're going to be painting and tearing up stuff," I said. "You should probably wear something you don't care much about."

"Don't be silly." Jessica laughed. "It's national TV." If she said that one more time, I was going to hang up on her, I swore. "What you do is wear something that looks like you're trying to be casual but you accidentally look cute. That's the key."

I pulled the phone away from my ear and stared at it. Was this the normal type of conversation Jessica and I had? Not that it wasn't fun. It just seemed like there should be something more important to talk about than how we looked.

"So, anyway," Jessica said. "Do you think Vi is mad at you?"

Those words pulled me out of my thoughts. It was the one thing I wanted to talk about right now. Maybe Jess would have some thoughts on how I could win Vi back to my side.

"She said I wasn't the person she thought I was," I told her.

Jessica was silent for a moment, probably thinking that one over. "What does that mean?"

"I'm too gossipy."

I stopped short of telling her about our no-gossip deal. I don't know why. It would have been perfectly okay to tell her at this point, since Vi was probably never speaking to me again anyway, but I was embarrassed about it. I couldn't even go thirty days without gossiping. What kind of person was I?

"Too gossipy?" Jessica said the words as though they were completely crazy.

"I talk about other people and spread secrets," I said, trying to throw the blame back on me. The last thing I wanted was to make everyone mad at Vi. I was the one in the wrong here.

"Don't we all?" Jessica asked. "And what's wrong with that, anyway? It's human nature."

"It's wrong," I said. "Especially when it hurts others. How would you feel if people were talking about you behind your back?"

We'd all had this conversation before, and Sarah had said she was sure people did talk about us. That didn't make it right, though.

"I wouldn't like it," Jessica replied. "Chelsea Tucker calls me 'frizz head' right to my face. I've tried every kind of conditioner, mousse, gel . . . you name it that my mom can find, and my hair's still frizzy. I can't help it."

"My point exactly," I said. "Talking about people hurts them."

"Not if they don't know about it," Jessica said.

"But they don't have to know about it. The point is, *we* know about it. We have to find a way to be nicer to people. We have to find a way to be more like . . ."

I hesitated. Did I dare say it? Oh, why not? I had nothing to lose at this point.

"Vi," I finished.

"Vi?" she asked. "You're saying we need to be more like her?"

"Yes."

"No, thanks. Talk about a bore. She just sits around drawing all the time. Talking about people is more fun."

I wanted to defend Vi, but Jessica's words had me too shocked to respond. As she started talking about what she thought Chelsea would do once cameras were on her, my mind couldn't let go of what Jessica had said. What Vi had said. And the contrast between the two.

It just confirmed what I'd already been thinking: Vi was right. She'd been right all along.

Seeing Vi the next morning felt like someone had punched me in the stomach. She was at her locker with Kelsey and another girl I recognized from elementary school. Both were supersmart, and, like Vi, both had better things to do than gossip about some TV show coming to our school.

I tried not to look over at them as I stepped up to my locker and turned the combination. The good news was that they were so caught up in whatever they were reading in a book Kelsey was holding, they'd never see me.

I pulled my books out of my locker, closed it, and turned to look at the group gathered down the hall. Did Vi think they were better friends than I was? *I*, who had been there for her since we were born? Impossible.

She'd just forgotten. She'd forgotten it all. There had to be some way to remind her, and I had a feeling it had something to do with *24-Hour Makeover*. If *24-Hour Makeover* was coming here—if I hadn't blown it for everyone—maybe I could somehow make things right between me and Vi. It would be the only way to get her back. I just had to show Vi that I would do anything for her, while somehow finding a way to stop myself from gossiping. I'd work with Miss Golden and make this work out for Vi somehow.

I wasn't sure how yet, but I had to try.

"I need to speak with Miss Golden."

I was standing in the principal's office, speaking to whoever would listen. They'd told me I couldn't see Mr. Shelly, who was in his office with the door closed, so the plan was to stand here until someone got tired enough of listening to me to open the door and tell Mr. Shelly I was here.

Or call someone to pull me out of here.

"She's not here," the woman behind the desk said. "I haven't seen her since last week."

I saw her yesterday, but that didn't necessarily mean anything. She could have bypassed the office altogether when she entered the school. But as I stood there, staring down the woman whose name I didn't know who usually sat way back at the back wall, working away, doubts started creeping in. Maybe Miss Golden wasn't coming back.

It wasn't a crazy thing to assume, since the entire school was pretty much buzzing about *24-Hour Makeover* by now, thanks to me. The fact that word of their show had gotten out could very well have scared them off. They might have a rule that they didn't want to shoot in a school where the students knew they were around. Didn't some reality shows have that?

As I stood there, weighing my options, the door to Mr. Shelly's office opened and he stuck his head out. "Miss Evans, so nice to see you again."

He said it in a way that told me it wasn't nice to see me again. But I was definitely glad to see him. He could answer my questions.

"I'm looking for Miss Golden."

Mr. Shelly didn't look surprised by that at all. He did, however, look like he didn't want it shouted out in front of everyone in his office. He stepped back, holding his door open and ushering me inside. I rushed into his office before he could change his mind.

No, Ashley Golden wasn't hiding in there, nor was her camera crew. I didn't really expect they were. They'd probably do their work when school wasn't in session.

"Please, have a seat," Mr. Shelly said. He closed the door behind him and took his place behind his large, old wooden desk. Maybe *24-Hour Makeover* could start with his office. I was sure Miss Golden thought of that while she was talking to him. "What can I help you with today, Miss Evans?"

He knew my name now and wasn't afraid to use it. I wasn't sure having the principal know your name was a good thing. I took a deep breath and stated my case.

"My friend Vi Lakewood is an aspiring interior designer," I rushed to say. "She's really good. She redid her brother's room and is now redoing her own bedroom. I've seen her paint walls, pick out carpets, and do all kinds of great work."

Mr. Shelly was giving me that look now. It was a look I

knew all too well. He had no idea where I was going with all this. I had to just spit it out.

"I know who Miss Golden is."

He didn't look surprised at that, which surprised me. Okay, so it was easy enough to search someone's last name and figure out who the person was these days, but I'd counted on Mr. Shelly not figuring out that much. If he knew that I knew who Miss Golden was, did that mean . . . ?

"Who is she?" he asked, clasping his hands together in front of him on his desk. He was waiting patiently for me to explain. He even had a slightly amused look on his face. Like he couldn't wait to watch me dig myself in deeper.

"She's with a reality show called *24-Hour Makeover*. She's here to redo this school. She's specifically interested in the language arts wing and creating a break area for us."

He made no expression at all at that news. He just continued to look at me as if waiting to hear more. I told myself that just because he wasn't surprised that I knew who Miss Golden was, it didn't mean he knew the whole school knew who Miss Golden was. But I wasn't so sure about that.

I decided to focus on what I'd come in here to say. "Vi is, like, *24-Hour Makeover*'s biggest fan," I continued. "She could tell you every place they've been. She could probably also tell you that they usually get people to help out with the work. In this case, I think it would be better for the students to help out than the teachers. It would make the people watching at home connect more with the show."

I'd worked hard preparing this argument, learning everything I could find out online about the show. When I was practicing, I'd assumed Miss Golden would be the one I'd be talking to about it. If I had to go through Mr. Shelly first, though, I'd do it.

But Mr. Shelly wasn't talking. He was still staring at me, and the look on his face wasn't a good one. Had I said something wrong? Oh, I knew what it was. He wanted me to talk to Miss Golden first.

"I could talk to Miss Golden about all this, but we aren't supposed to know, right?" I asked. "I mean, we could get in trouble if word gets out, I assume."

Those words broke his silence. "Miss Evans, I can assure you that we appreciate your input," Mr. Shelly said. "But the participants in the work have already been chosen."

What? *No.*

Okay, I admit it. I panicked. I had been fully planning to use *24-Hour Makeover* to win my best friend back. If I didn't have the show, what did I have?

Nothing. Vi would never speak to me again, and the

rest of the school would hate me for getting their hopes up about all this. I'd be a total social outcast. I wouldn't even be able to get anyone to read the *Troy Tattler* anymore.

"Are they teachers?" I asked, my voice far more high pitched than I meant for it to be. "Teachers get to do everything. This school isn't about teachers. It's about students."

Mr. Shelly's brow furrowed and I knew I was pushing it. Oh well. I'd already gone this far, so I might as well keep going.

"My friend Vi is really good," I continued. "She could work circles around any of these teachers, but you aren't even giving her a chance. It's not fair."

I knew I sounded like a big baby at that point, but I didn't care. The image of all those teachers standing in the language arts wing with their hammers and nails got to me. Cameras would be zooming around them, showing how much they cared about the students of this school. But what nobody at home would know was that the teachers were just hogging the spotlight, taking it away from the kids.

When Mr. Shelly spoke, his voice was calm, especially in contrast to my half-hysterical ramblings. "Miss Evans, do you know what happens when people make assumptions?"

His question threw me for a second. "No?"

It was a question, not an answer. I waited for him to

continue. He stared down at his hands, and I wondered if he was trying to gather patience.

"People spread incorrect information," he finally told me. "I have not yet said who the participants are, yet you're already making assumptions, aren't you?"

His words had silenced me. I couldn't seem to speak. All I could do was stare at him as the things he was saying sank in.

"For instance, I did not say that those participants had been notified, nor did I say the school had chosen those participants, did I?" Mr. Shelly continued. He was looking directly at me now, and it made me want to sink into a hole.

I shook my head.

"I'm well aware that the word has gotten out about *24-Hour Makeover*. I'm also aware that you produce a publication called the *Troy Tattler*. Is this information correct?"

I opened my mouth to defend myself, but what could I say? Not only did I write and publish the *Troy Tattler* but I was responsible for the word getting out about the show. I had no defense.

"If one were to draw conclusions, one would *assume* you spread that little piece of gossip," Mr. Shelly said. "Especially since you were the only student who met

Miss Golden. But I wouldn't assume any of that. Do you know why?"

I had a feeling that whether I knew why or not, Mr. Shelly fully planned to blaze forward with his speech. So I just sat there quietly.

"Because making assumptions gets you into trouble," Mr. Shelly finished. He sat back in his chair and looked at me. "I have a feeling you're figuring that out now, aren't you?"

"Yes," I said. My throat was suddenly very dry, making my voice sound like it was coming through sandpaper. "I'm sorry."

And I was. I'd made such a mess of things, and I wasn't sure how to make it right. It seemed like the harder I tried, the worse it got, until I felt like I was sinking deeper and deeper and deeper. . . .

Mr. Shelly stood and walked around his desk. "The funny thing is, *you* were actually on the list to help out, but now the entire future of the project is in jeopardy. Do you know why?"

I bit my lip. "I think so," I admitted. I was the reason. Whether he knew it or not, it was all because of me.

"Miss Golden does not yet know word has gotten out, but it's only a matter of time," he said. "We were expected to reveal what was really going on the morning of the shoot. The instructions were to tell the entire school we were doing this project and anyone who wanted to participate could show up, and that was when it would be announced that it would be televised."

That made sense. If they asked the school to show up and work hard all day, a completely different group of people would show up than if they asked everyone to show up and be on national TV. I could totally see why my big mouth could blow it all.

"Miss Evans." Mr. Shelly said the words sternly, a frown creasing his forehead. He would never say that he knew I spread the gossip, but I was pretty sure he knew I had. And, like every other grown-up, he wanted me to learn my lesson. He wanted to scare me into thinking that I'd blown it for everyone when maybe I hadn't.

But maybe I had. . . .

"Please don't punish Vi because of me," I begged. "She knew nothing about all of this. In fact, she's mad at me because she says I can't stop gossiping. She doesn't believe in gossip. Vi's the greatest person ever and she'll be really, really good on the show."

Mr. Shelly was at the door by then, his hand on the doorknob. "I don't know who this Vi is—"

"Vivienne Lakewood," I said, hoping like crazy I wasn't messing it up by telling him that. He might head back to his desk and write her name on a bad list or something. I stood and walked over to where he was standing. "She'll make this school look good, I promise."

He paused, his hand still on the doorknob. "I don't think you understand what I'm saying." He looked me directly in the eye. "This has nothing to do with your friend. It's not up to me. If the show finds out people knew about it—"

"They won't find out," I pleaded. "I promise. I'll make sure everyone acts surprised. Please give us this chance."

"It's out of my hands now."

I didn't know what that meant, but it was clear that he had no plans to tell me. He opened the door and gestured for me to leave, giving me that one last look that told me the same thing Vi's looks had told me lately. He was disappointed in me.

I couldn't blame him. Or Vi. I was more disappointed in myself than anyone else could ever be.

Chapter Thirteen

"WHAT'S WITH VI?"

"She's mad at Maddie."

"She's not mad at us. Why isn't she sitting with us?"

This conversation was going on around me as I sat, quietly eating my pizza at lunch the next day. Vi continued to make it clear that she wasn't speaking to me. Maybe ever again. I, meanwhile, wasn't sure how I could make things right between us.

"Sitting with us means sitting with Maddie, and Vi can't stand to be around her right now."

They all looked over at me. I wanted to shrink down in my seat. Was the whole school mad at me now? They'd really be mad when they found out that because I couldn't stop gossiping, the whole *24-Hour Makeover* thing would be canceled.

"Vi doesn't believe in gossip," Sydney said, turning to look at Jessica and Sarah. "Haven't you ever noticed? She refuses to talk about other people. She doesn't approve. All you have to do is look at her when Maddie's gossiping."

I gasped. "When *I'm* gossiping? We all gossip."

"Guys . . . ," Jessica said.

"You talk, we listen," Sarah interrupted. "That's the way it usually goes. Half of what you say doesn't even come true. You just tell us something you overheard someone say."

Now Sarah was turning on me? "I always tell you if it's something I don't know for sure," I said. "You guys tell everyone else like it's fact."

"I don't think we do that," Jessica said. She looked at Sydney. "Do we do that?"

"You're all missing the point," Sarah said. "We're talking about Vi and the fact that she's sitting over there by herself."

"She's not by herself," Sydney corrected. "She's with the brainiacs."

We all turned to look and, sure enough, Vi was seated at the table where all the smart people sat. The mathletes and honor students were all talking to her as if she'd been hanging out with them forever. I felt a little stab of jealousy.

She was my best friend. So why did she already look like she was so happy with her new friends?

Finally, I'd had enough. Everyone was turning on me and my best friend had moved on to other friends. I had nothing to lose. So I told the truth.

"Vi challenged me to go thirty days with no gossip," I said. "That's why I stopped putting the *Troy Tattler* out. That's why I haven't been gossiping as much. I was doing it to save my friendship with Vi."

They all stared at me without speaking. Finally, Sarah looked at the other two before saying something.

"She said she wouldn't be friends with you anymore if you didn't stop gossiping?" Sarah asked. "What kind of friend is that?"

"She was trying to make me a better person," I answered. I knew I was supposed to be defending myself here, not Vi, but I couldn't let them blame Vi for this. "She thinks I need to look at why I talk about other people and how much it hurts them."

"It doesn't hurt anyone if they don't know about it," Jessica said.

"I guess Vi thinks it hurts *me*," I said. "It makes me a worse person."

Sydney tossed her half-eaten cookie down on her plate.

"That's ridiculous." She sighed. "Everyone talks about other people. If we didn't, what would we talk about?"

"TV, movies . . . ," Sarah said. She started to list more, but Jessica spoke up.

"But even that's no fun if you can only say nice things. 'Did you see Rachel McAdams at the awards last night? She had the prettiest dress and her hair looked so perfect. . . .'"

"That's how we talk about Rachel McAdams," Sarah said, confused.

"But imagine if we talked that way about everyone," Jessica told us. "How boring."

"How *sad* that we have nothing else to talk about but other people," I said. "Maybe we should find something else to talk about."

They were all staring at me now. *Me*, the queen of gossip, arguing against talking about people. It surprised me, too. But I'd seen how hard it was to keep from gossiping around here.

"I don't think it's all me." I sat up a little straighter. I felt more confident now. I looked Sydney directly in the eye as I spoke. "I've spent almost a week trying not to gossip, and everyone else filled in the blanks. I never even said *24-Hour Makeover* was coming here. Jessica said it, in a question."

"I did not," Jessica said. "*You* told *us*."

"Actually, Maddie's right."

Sydney was the one who said that, surprising all of us. Once we were all staring at her, she continued.

Sydney sighed. "I've been watching Maddie for Vi."

Now she had our full attention. Especially mine. Sydney was the "way" Vi had of knowing if I gossiped? It made sense, but knowing two of my friends had some kind of agreement about me made me angry. And embarrassed.

"What?" Sarah asked. "Why did you do that?"

"Because Vi asked me to." Sydney shrugged. "I was supposed to try to get her to gossip, but I was so impressed that she was actually going through with it, I couldn't do it. So I mostly just watched her.

"And . . . ?" Sarah asked.

"And she's right," Sydney said. "Most of the gossip that came out was from everyone else filling in the blanks. When Maddie didn't talk, people would talk for her. Like the time we were asking about *24-Hour Makeover*." Sydney looked over at Jessica. "You're the one who pieced that together and asked Maddie about it. She didn't even answer at first."

Jessica was speechless. And that wasn't a normal thing. I felt like I had to say something to make things right.

"Vi's right. We don't have to gossip. We could find more useful things to talk about."

"Than what's going on in school?" Jessica asked. "Like what?"

"I don't know, but we have to work on it." I stood, gathering my mostly empty tray and my books. "I'm going to the library to figure out what. Anyone want to join me?"

They all stared up at me. I could tell from looking at each one of them that they thought I'd lost my mind. As soon as I stepped away from this table, they'd start talking about me. For once, I didn't care. I turned and walked toward the library, deciding that whatever they thought of me was no longer my problem. From now on, I was focusing on what was important.

Maybe that was the progress Vi had been talking about.

"All seventh graders, please report to the gym for a special assembly."

I was leaving the library, two books about the history of our town in my hand, when the announcement came over the loudspeaker. The bell had rung a few seconds earlier, so students were just starting to pour into the hallway from classrooms. It didn't matter what grade a student was in, when the announcement came on, everyone had the same expression.

What's that all about?

I made a sharp right turn to head toward the gym. I

had a feeling this was about *24-Hour Makeover*, and I felt a huge weight in the pit of my stomach at the thought of it. This was where we were going to be called into the assembly to be told someone had gossiped and blown the most exciting thing that had ever happened at Troy Middle. Mr. Shelly and the teachers may have no idea who had leaked the news, but half the students in seventh grade knew. And they'd all turn their glaring eyes on me.

Never mind that other people had gossiped too. Never mind that other people had filled in the blanks when all I had done was hint there might be something going on. My friends at lunch had echoed what everyone else in school would say if anyone pointed out that they gossiped too. They didn't think *they* gossiped. They thought they just listened to me.

I suppose I deserved all that. The whole school could hate me for all I cared. The important thing was that Vi would be sitting there, in the auditorium, next to her new friends. She'd hear all of it, and it would just confirm what she'd thought all along. I wasn't a good friend. She was right to stop speaking to me.

Since I was close by, I was one of the first people in the gym. Whenever we had an assembly, Vi and I always sat in the same area, so I headed there. Maybe she'd come up and sit, mad at me or not, out of habit. A few minutes later, as the bleachers filled up, I started to feel really silly sitting in the center toward the back with nobody around me.

Luckily, Jessica, Sarah, and Sydney came in and found me. At least I hadn't completely messed things up with them. They even talked about a few of the people coming in—what they were wearing, who they were dating, that sort of thing—and didn't seem to mind that I didn't join in.

"See if you can get Vi to sit with us," I said to Jessica the second I spotted Vi coming in. She had her new friends with her, so it was doubtful, but there was an entire row in front of us that was empty. It would be far easier for them to sit there than anywhere else.

As Vi's gaze scanned the bleachers, it momentarily landed on me. She looked, for just a second, like she might wave to me and come up and sit down. My heart fluttered and I smiled, my hand automatically gesturing for her to come here. But just as I thought she might start up this way, someone said something and she turned away, following the group of brainiacs to a seat near the locker rooms.

"So much for that," Sydney said.

I didn't really have time to dwell on that, since Sarah chose that time to have a semi-meltdown. She grabbed Sydney's arm so hard, Sydney cried out.

"There he is, there he is, there he is," Sarah began chanting.

I followed the direction of her gaze and saw Aiden. The reason she was freaking out was that he was walking this way. He was climbing the steps leading up to where we sat, staring straight at Sarah as he walked. I would probably be freaking out too.

"What do I do?" Sarah asked.

"What are you talking about?" Sydney asked, pulling away from Sarah's grabs. "Just be cool."

Sarah did exactly the opposite, sitting there stiffly, staring straight ahead as Aiden and one of his friends plopped down on the bleacher directly in front of us. He turned and said hi to her, and the hi she gave back sounded like something that came from an excited four-year-old.

I rolled my eyes as he turned back around. What was the big deal? She already knew he liked her, so why be all nervous? Plus, she'd had a boyfriend before, so wasn't she used to this stuff?

"Testing, one-two-three," Mr. Shelly said into the microphone. The noise in the gym seemed to get louder instead of quieter at that. I didn't get it. Wasn't everyone as anxious to hear what this assembly was about as I was?

"We're all in trouble," Sydney whispered, leaning over so

only I could hear. "He's going to tell us *24-Hour Makeover* was scared off by all the gossip."

I stared at her, my eyes wide. That was exactly what was about to happen. How had she known? Had someone said something to her? I swallowed against the lump in my throat and turned back to survey the scene on the gym floor in front of us. Mr. Shelly stood in front of the mic with all the teachers gathered in a straight line behind him. None of them had a grim, depressed face. If we were all in trouble, wouldn't some of them look a little mad? Wouldn't they be scanning the audience to see who the bad guy was who had ruined Troy Middle's chances at national fame?

Even weirder, Miss Golden was standing off to the side, and she didn't look mad either. She *was* scanning the audience, but she had a big smile on her face. People giving bad news didn't smile, from what I'd noticed.

"Okay, everyone, could we pipe down a little?" Mr. Shelly said into the microphone. "We need to get you all back to class."

It seemed like the noise increased, which wasn't a surprise. Nobody was all that excited about getting back to class. Maybe he should try another trick.

When a couple of minutes passed with still no relief,

Ms. Hunter grabbed the mic from him. "Quiet!" she shouted, her voice echoing off the tall ceilings.

Within a few seconds, the noise had dulled to a small murmur. A couple of seconds more and Mr. Shelly had the quiet he needed. That was when my heart really started racing.

"We have a special guest with us here today at Troy Middle School," Mr. Shelly said. "And she's going to talk to us about an exciting new opportunity. Everyone, please welcome, from the popular cable show *24-Hour Makeover*, Ashley Golden."

Exciting. New. *Opportunity?*

I didn't get it. Was this some kind of trick? Get us all hopeful and then pull the rug out from under us? Tell us we were going to be on national TV and it was going to be so exciting and, yes, we were even going to get new paint and floors and stuff . . . all for free. Then, once everyone was all excited, step in and tell us that because someone had let the secret out, the whole deal was off?

Miss Golden's smile widened as she stepped in front of everyone. She wore a T-shirt and jeans, which made it look like she was ready to start working now. I wondered if she'd help out on the project. Or did she just come in, set it up, and head back to Hollywood?

After a long pause, Miss Golden started speaking. "How many of you take classes in the language arts wing?"

Hands went up all around me. Of course we did. Language arts was required for seventh graders. We were the only ones who ever used that wing, except for some eighth graders who had lockers down that way. I'd figured they stuck the seventh graders there because it was the worst part of the school. Sixth graders were new and they didn't want to scare them off, and eighth graders had paid their dues and deserved to have classes in nicer areas.

"How many of you think that wing could use a twenty-four-hour makeover?" Miss Golden said enthusiastically.

The enthusiasm caught on. People cheered. Some clapped. Even those who sat silently seemed to be buzzing with excitement. They knew something big was happening here.

"How many of you would like to see a break area take the place of that old deserted classroom at the end of the hall?" Miss Golden asked.

More cheering. I realized then that I was probably the only one in the whole place not cheering. I was just sitting there, staring at Miss Golden, feeling like my entire body was frozen in place. What was happening here?

"The TV show *24-Hour Makeover* will bring you that

and so much more," Miss Golden said. Now she sounded like a cheerleader. "And that's not even the best part."

No one cheered that time. Everyone was listening attentively, trying to figure out what came next. A big-screen TV? Built-in computers for checking e-mail? Free fresh-baked cookies any time of day?

"You get to help."

Miss Golden was looking at all of us, but it felt like she was looking right at me. I'm sure everyone else thought she was looking at them.

"Since the seventh graders use that hall the most, the seventh graders get to help," Miss Golden continued. "Just show up Saturday morning at six a.m., and we'll put you to work."

Mr. Shelly stepped forward and took the mic. "You aren't guaranteed to be filmed," he said, before handing the microphone back to her.

"The cameras will be rolling all day," Miss Golden said. "But we can't make any promises about what will end up in the final cut. Still . . . if you don't show up, you don't have a chance."

Mr. Shelly stepped up again. It sounded like he was telling her to tell us something else. She turned back to us, speaking into the mic.

"Yes, there is a catch," she admitted. "Only those who are here when we open the doors get to help. We'll let in whoever is outside the front doors, but then they will be locked."

Mr. Shelly took the mic again. "We'll have security guards, so don't get any ideas."

As I watched him step back and hand the microphone to Miss Golden, it hit me. He hadn't told her. Mr. Shelly had never said a word to *24-Hour Makeover* about the fact that students knew.

"But that's *still* not the best news," Miss Golden said.

Silence fell over the gym as everyone waited for the rest. My mind, meanwhile, was reeling. Of course Mr. Shelly hadn't told them that. He wasn't going to blow it for the school. In his office it had run through my mind that he might just be trying to scare me, and I'd been right. He'd never once said he was going to tell Miss Golden. I'd just been so mad at myself, I'd let myself believe I'd blown it. Instead, he'd kept his mouth shut, and I'd realized something very important about secrets and my complete horribleness at keeping them.

"We're having a contest for the best worker," Miss Golden was saying, her voice jerking me out of my thoughts. "The winner gets to come to Hollywood to help host the show about this school."

Everyone started talking again. A low rumble spread across the bleachers as everyone excitedly discussed what Miss Golden had just told us. A trip to Hollywood, but not only that—a trip to Hollywood to be on *TV*!

"Can we bring a friend on the trip if we win?" someone called out. I couldn't see who was doing the talking, but I frowned in the general direction of the voice.

"You can bring one parent or legal guardian," Miss Golden said. "Any other questions?"

I looked around. Nobody was raising a hand. Did I dare speak up? Did I have the nerve to open my big mouth after everything I'd done?

The answer was yes. For Vi, yes. I just had to avoid looking at Mr. Shelly and seeing his disapproving glare. I squeezed my eyes shut, I thought about Vi and how much this would mean to her, and before I could stop it, my arm shot up.

"Yes, Maddie?" Miss Golden said, her smile widening.

I winced. Now everyone was looking at me, waiting to see what I'd say. It probably didn't surprise them at all that I was asking a question.

"I was just wondering about the design," I spoke up to say. "What if someone is really good at picking out things? Could they help?"

"Are you volunteering?" Miss Golden asked.

"Not me," I said. "Someone else I know."

I shifted my gaze to where Vi was sitting. I couldn't see her from here, which meant she wasn't watching. But she could hear every word of this. I took a deep breath and returned my attention to Miss Golden.

"Speak to me after the assembly," Miss Golden said. "If there are no other questions, I'll turn it back over to Mr. Shelly."

Mr. Shelly gave us the usual routine about how he expected us to behave and make him proud and blah-blah-blah. I heard very little of it. I was too busy thinking up what I would say to Miss Golden.

As it turned out, there was a line to get to Miss Golden. I stepped in behind a group of girls who were trying to talk Miss Golden into letting them help with picking out things. No way. That was Vi's job.

I was so caught up in what they were saying, I didn't realize that Vi herself had stepped into place behind me until she spoke. "What exactly are you doing?"

I spun around, ready to defend myself. She wasn't about to attack me, though. She was simply waiting for an answer.

"Speaking to Miss Golden," I said. That was pretty obvious.

"About what?" she asked.

"Someone who would be perfect for helping them get all of this together" was all I said. I knew it was probably only a matter of seconds before I'd have to say exactly what I was trying to do. But before I could say anything, the girls in line in front of us left, and Miss Golden stepped over to stand in front of us.

"Is this Vi?" Miss Golden asked.

At that point, I not only didn't remember having mentioned Vi to Miss Golden but I couldn't believe that if I had, she'd even been listening. "Yes," I answered. I'd just have to wait to see what Miss Golden remembered about her.

"You must be the design expert," Miss Golden said. "I have to tell you, you have a great friend here."

Out of the corner of my eye, I saw Vi straighten a little. Would she say something against me to Miss Golden?

"She was telling me all about you," Miss Golden said. "This huge sales pitch about how great you'd be at helping with the makeover. You wouldn't believe the trouble she went through to help you. Now *that's* a friend." Miss Golden shook her head. "I wish I had a friend like that."

Vi looked down. Her shoulders were slumped now. I wanted to argue that as much as I was a good friend, I kept messing up. If I could just walk around with duct tape over my mouth all the time, I'd be a *great* friend.

"I want both of you," Miss Golden said.

She reached back and tapped Mr. Shelly on the shoulder. He turned around with a smile on his face, but when he saw me, that smile fell.

"These two are best friends," Miss Golden told him. "I think it would make for great TV to maybe hone in on them a little Saturday morning. Can you both be here at six a.m.?"

"Miss Evans won't be participating," Mr. Shelly said.

It seemed to take Miss Golden a second to realize that *I* was Miss Evans. She looked at me, her brow furrowing, and turned to Mr. Shelly.

"Why not?" Miss Golden said.

I'd expected this. I knew Mr. Shelly was mad at me for telling everyone about *24-Hour Makeover*. I didn't plan to help anyway. I didn't deserve to help. I'd stay home Saturday while everyone else had fun, and be happy knowing Vi was realizing her lifelong dream of being on her favorite TV show.

"Miss Evans knows what she did," Mr. Shelly replied.

He wouldn't say what I'd done because if he did, he could jeopardize the entire show. Instead, he gave me a grim look and turned around to continue his conversation.

Vi, on the other hand, had no issue with saying what I'd done. "Maddie has a bit of a problem with her mouth," she told Miss Golden without looking at me. "Seems she can't keep a secret. She—"

"I'm a gossip," I interrupted quickly, before Vi said anything more. If Vi let it slip that students knew about *24-Hour Makeover*, the whole thing could be toast. Now that everyone officially knew, what was the harm in keeping it a secret a little longer, right?

Vi laughed. "A gossip? She told everyone about you being here."

Miss Golden blinked. "She told everyone about me being here?"

"Yes," Vi said with a nod. "She looked you up online and figured out you were with *24-Hour Makeover*. All of these people probably already knew who you were when you made your announcement. Big surprise, huh?"

That whole tirade had gotten Mr. Shelly's attention. He'd stopped everything to turn around and look at us. All the blood seemed to have drained from his face as he stared directly at Miss Golden. Miss Golden, on the other hand, was still smiling. I don't think she got it.

"Interesting," Miss Golden said. She looked at me like

she had newfound respect for me, which was weird. And completely undeserved. Then she asked something that surprised me. "Nobody told you to keep it a secret, though?"

"No," I answered, lowering my head. "But that doesn't excuse it. I tried to keep it a secret and I goofed it all up."

"You're thirteen."

With those two words, my head lifted. Being thirteen was no excuse, but I wanted to hear what Miss Golden had to say. Instead, Mr. Shelly broke in.

"Discretion is important," Mr. Shelly said. "Miss Evans is the publisher of a newsletter called the *Troy Tattler*. You can't tell her anything without it being spread all over school, the Internet—even the evening news."

That last part was a huge exaggeration, but Miss Golden probably knew that. "Hmph," Miss Golden said. She was still giving me that interested look.

"It's something I'm working on," I insisted. I looked over at Vi, who rolled her eyes. I added, more insistently, "I *am*."

"Then why does the entire school know about *24-Hour Makeover*?" Vi asked.

"Ask Sydney," I said. "People were guessing what was going on. I tried not to tell them—"

"So," Miss Golden interrupted. "If I needed to get the

word out about something, it sounds like you're the person to talk to."

Both Vi and I turned to face her. Mr. Shelly was looking at her now too. We were all waiting to find out where she was going with this.

"I think this could be useful," Miss Golden said, turning back to Mr. Shelly. "We need someone who can promote *24-Hour Makeover*, especially once the episode is about to air. We've been trying to reach a younger age group, and someone like Maddie here can do much better than our publicists at posting things like this on social media sites."

Mr. Shelly looked puzzled. I was afraid to look at Vi. All of this was really confusing.

"Do you have a cell phone with a camera?" Miss Golden asked me. "Of course you do. I saw it the day I met you, in Mr. Shelly's office. How would you feel about taking pictures Saturday and posting some things online for us?"

I didn't know what it involved, but I didn't have to know. "I'd love to!" I practically shouted.

"Wait a second," Mr. Shelly broke in. "You're telling me you're actually going to encourage her to spread the word about your show?"

"Sure." Miss Golden shrugged as if to say, *Why not?*

"Because that behavior should be punished," Mr. Shelly

said. "It's because of Maddie that the entire school knew about this before you showed up. This breaches the confidentiality."

"There's nothing confidential about *24-Hour Makeover*," Miss Golden said with a dismissive wave. "Plus, I guarantee she's not the only gossip around here. One person can't spread something like that on her own. I'll make you a deal. If you'll let her participate Saturday, I'll make sure she works hard. Deal?"

Mr. Shelly looked at me, then at Miss Golden. "Deal," he agreed. "But I want to see this one covered in paint by the end of the day."

Miss Golden shrugged as Mr. Shelly walked away. Then she turned back to the two of us.

"Be here Saturday at six a.m.," she told us. "And don't be late."

Miss Golden turned to speak to someone else, which was when the hard part began. Vi and I were left alone to talk to each other. This was my chance to state my case. But Vi turned and walked off. Before she did, though, I thought I saw something in her eyes. Gratitude. That had to be a good sign, right?

Chapter Fourteen

THERE WAS A REASON THE GROWN-UPS HAD TOLD US that if we weren't here by six a.m., we wouldn't be a part of the show. Six a.m. was tough, especially on a Saturday. Saturdays were for sleeping in and hanging out all day. Saturdays weren't for bicycling to Troy Middle School in your old jeans and tennis shoes, hoping you made it in time.

It was actually five fifty-five when I parked my bike at the rack, but I wasn't the first person to show up. Not by a long shot. The sidewalk in front of the door was packed with students. There were cars pulling up too, still dropping students off. I pulled out my camera and started snapping pictures. If Miss Golden wanted me to post this everywhere, I may as well start now.

"Maddie, over here!"

I heard Jessica calling out to me, but I couldn't see her. Not in this crowd. I was starting toward the end of what I assumed was some kind of line when I saw movement off to the side. Jessica was jumping up and down.

"Maddie." Jump. "This way." Jump. "We saved you . . ."

I couldn't hear her last few words as she dropped back down again, but I could piece it together. She was saying they'd saved me a place.

"Maddie!"

Now Chelsea was calling out to me. She was just a few feet away, near the end of the line. She was giving me her biggest, brightest smile, and it made me smile back.

But then I heard Jessica again. I stopped and looked from Chelsea to Jessica. Sydney rose up on tiptoe and started waving too. My friends. Then I looked at Chelsea and saw someone who had never been my friend. She'd only ever been nice to me when she thought I had information she might want.

I turned and started in the direction that felt most natural to me. I squeezed through the crowd and a few seconds later was standing next to two of my three closest friends in the world.

"This is so exciting," Jessica said. "Aren't you excited?"

I nodded, thinking that was a silly question. Of course I

was excited. We were all excited. Jessica was looking at me with this huge, hopeful smile on her face, though, so I tried hard to get to her level of cheerleaderish happiness.

"Can't wait," I said, pasting on a huge smile. In truth, I was too nervous to be excited. I didn't know what Miss Golden had planned for me and Vi. Mostly, though, I was worried about Vi. Could I somehow make this work so we were friends again?

The front doors to the school had obviously opened because the crowd suddenly started pushing toward the school. I went with it and just hoped I wouldn't be trampled before we got inside.

Once through the doors, everyone seemed to be heading in the same direction—toward the language arts wing. I wanted to slow everything down. It was all going so quickly, I didn't have time to figure it all out. Plus, I needed to find Vi.

I couldn't find Vi *or* Miss Golden. Everyone was spread around the annex, being given instructions and materials. Lots of paint cans and brushes and those tray things to pour paint into. So we were painting over the painted brick? Someone pulled a ladder in and gathered some students around to talk about the ceiling.

Somehow I'd gotten separated from Jessica and Sydney as the crowd had pushed between us. As I was craning my neck to look for them, Chelsea stepped up next to me.

"Where are the cameras?" Chelsea asked. She was look-ing around too.

I shrugged. Why did she think I'd know?

"Can you get us on TV?" Kathina asked. Chelsea gave her a look, to which Kathina responded by lowering her gaze to the floor.

"What Kathina means is, do you think that pretty producer lady could get us on camera working with you?" Chelsea asked. "You know, since you and Vi are going to be the stars and all."

I looked at Kathina, then at Emma, who was trailing along after them. The three of them were only being nice to me because they thought I was going to be the star of this thing. That was it. I had no more to say to them.

I spun around to rush off in search of Vi and nearly ran directly into a camera. Behind it was a guy, and next to him, a guy with a microphone he was holding above all of us. There were other people too, all of whom traveled in a large clump behind the camera.

Wow. How could anyone have a conversation like nothing out of the ordinary was happening with all of this going on?

"Hi, everyone!"

I was so busy nearly running down the camera crew, I didn't see Jilly zoom around them. Jilly was *24-Hour Makeover*'s star. She worked on everything with the help of a crew of assorted muscle-bound guys. Jilly looked even more amazing in person than she did on TV.

Everything stopped. I was pretty sure most of these people had no idea who Jilly was. I mean, how many seventh graders watched home remodeling shows? But Jilly was the type of person you looked at. Everything about her looked better than anyone you normally saw.

"I'm Jilly Clark," she announced. Funny that even as small as she was, she could speak loudly enough to be heard all the way down the hall. "I host *24-Hour Makeover*. We're going to have some fun today."

People cheered. I couldn't help but get caught up in the excitement. It felt like something big was happening here . . . and I was part of it.

"I need to see someone named Vivienne Lakewood?" Jilly said. She was reading off a slip of paper she'd been holding and looking around.

Vivienne. *Vi!* I stood on tiptoe to look around. No sign of Vi. She would have stepped forward by now, wouldn't she?"

"Okay, Emma Mayfield?" Jilly said.

"Me!" Emma pushed her way through the people in

front of her and stood eagerly in front of Jilly. It was a little nauseating.

"Luke Summer?" Jilly continued.

Luke climbed down from his ladder and started toward Jilly. I, meanwhile, was starting to panic. Jilly had already called two other names, and Vi wasn't answering. Had she gotten stuck outside the school? I pulled my cell phone out of my pocket, stepped away from the camera and the crowd, and called her.

The phone rang so many times, I was sure it was about to go to voice mail. I didn't know what I'd do at that point. A voice mail wouldn't help me get her in here, where she needed to be. I was about to call her over and over until she answered, but she picked up on the second try.

"Hello?" She sounded groggy. Like she'd been asleep.

"Vi? Where are you?"

Silence on the other end. She'd figured out it was me, but would that make her hang up?

"Maddie. What time is it?"

"After six o'clock," I said. "You're missing everything."

I'm sure my panic was coming over the line, but I couldn't help it. This was probably the biggest day of Vi's life and she'd overslept?

If we'd still been BFFs, this wouldn't have happened. I

would have spent the night at her house or she would have spent the night at mine. We would have set seven alarms if that was what it took to make sure we got up in time. For backup, we probably also would have had her mom wake us and maybe had Jessica or Sydney do a wake-up call. That was how Vi was.

"My alarm must not have gone off," Vi said. "It's too late."

I knew that sound in her voice. She sounded like she was about to be sick. She was right. It was too late. I remembered what Miss Golden had said about the doors to the school locking at six a.m. and absolutely no one else being let in. I'd seen the security guard stationed at the door when we'd entered and knew they were serious about that. There was no way to get Vi in here at this point unless I appealed to Miss Golden. Even then, knowing adults, she'd say if she made an exception for Vi, she'd have to make an exception for everyone else standing out there.

As I hesitated, I heard Jilly tell the small group she'd gathered that they were all going to Pro Hardware in town with her to pick out materials for the remodel. That was it. The perfect way to get Vi in.

"You were chosen," I told Vi. "Jilly Clark just called your name."

"She did?"

Vi no longer sounded sad. I knew I'd gotten her attention when I mentioned Jilly Clark's name. Jilly Clark was her hero. Her idol. Vi was the only reason I knew who Jilly Clark even was.

"She's standing right here in front of me," I told her. "And just two minutes ago, she said your name. You were the first name she called."

"Called? For what?"

"She picked out four people to go with her to Pro Hardware," I said. "They're leaving now. You were one of the four, but you aren't here."

"Oh," Vi said, that sick sound in her voice again as she realized she'd just missed one of the best opportunities ever.

"Go to Pro Hardware," I instructed, speaking quietly as I watched Jilly leaving, the camera crew rushing after her. "Get there as quickly as you can. Jilly's on her way."

I was still putting my phone away when I saw Jessica and Sydney waving me over. They were standing near the paint buckets. I grabbed a paintbrush and started painting.

Cameras seemed to be following me everywhere I went, but I tried to ignore them. We'd all been told to pretend they weren't there, but I couldn't help but notice that people were all too aware of them. Whenever a camera would come our way, for instance, Sydney would suddenly start talking louder and working harder than she did when the cameras weren't around. I, meanwhile, was falling behind because I had to stop every few minutes to take another picture and post it to three different sites.

"Where's that producer woman?" Sydney whispered. A camera was on the group next to us, so I guess she didn't want her question to be picked up by the large microphones.

I looked around again. I'd seen no sign of Miss Golden all morning, but now that I was looking, I found her. It was no wonder I hadn't noticed her. Surprisingly, she was in jeans and an oversize sweatshirt, painting with a group at the far end of the hall. I wouldn't have thought she would help out with the remodel, but I guess they needed all the hands they could get at this point.

Around the time we were about to break for lunch—they'd brought in pizzas for everyone—Vi showed up. She was with Emma and the two others, but there was no sign of Jilly. Miss Golden sent a group of guys out to the parking lot to bring in the materials they'd bought.

Vi and the others mingled in with the crowd, which had now gathered near the front to prepare to head to the cafeteria for lunch. I was too far from the back to even see Vi, but I was so happy she'd made it in, I didn't care. In the brief glimpse I'd gotten of her, she looked happy, and that was all that mattered. After spending the morning shopping with her idol, I was sure the rest of this was icing on the cake.

"After lunch, our team of four will meet to draw up the master plan for the break area," Miss Golden announced. "The rest of you will keep working. Enjoy your lunch."

I looked around as the crowd moved in one large mass toward the cafeteria. At some point, they'd replaced the old, discolored ceiling tiles with new white ones. The walls were done—the top half was bright white and the bottom half was a deep golden yellow. I still didn't get the master plan. It looked cleaner and less run-down, but it was still just a hallway. I didn't see how we could make it something people would ooh and ahh over on TV.

"This is where the fun starts," Jessica said as we entered the cafeteria.

I assumed she was talking about eating pizza, but she started in on all the exciting things we could do to make the walls of the hallway look better. Finally I had to stop her.

"What are you talking about?" I asked.

"The stencils," she said with a shrug. She leaned forward to look at my face. We were in line for pizza by then. I figured by the time we got to the front of the line, all the good slices would be gone. "Have you never watched *24-Hour Makeover?*"

"I watch it all the time," I replied.

Well, in truth, I'd only recently started really watching it. It was on every time I was with Vi, but most of the time I was only halfway watching to keep Vi happy. I'd be checking e-mail on my phone or reading one of Vi's design magazines or picking on her little brother.

"Maddie doesn't know about the stencils," Jessica said to someone over my shoulder. I turned around, figuring I'd see Sydney, but instead it was Vi.

I tried not to show how excited I was to have her standing there. Scared, too. What if she was here to tell me how mad she was at me or something?

"Huh?" Vi asked.

"Maddie says she watches *24-Hour Makeover*," Jessica said. "But she doesn't know about the stencils."

"You remember the stencils," Vi said to me. "They always let the people who will be using a building put a personal touch on it. Usually that's by letting them paint something on the walls. Thank you."

That last part was a complete change of subject. I knew from the way her eyes were lit up that she was happy. Really happy.

"You're welcome." I smiled. I didn't know which thing specifically she was thanking me for, but I was so glad she was looking at me like a friend again, I didn't care.

"Isn't this the most exciting day ever?" Jessica asked. "We're going to be on TV."

Vi's smile fell. "I hope not."

Vi didn't want to be on TV. I'd learned that about her during all this. I guess it made sense. Vi had never been one to try to hog the spotlight, instead standing back and watching everyone else. Having a camera shoved in her face wasn't her thing.

"Vi isn't into that," I explained. "She's more excited to learn new things and design something awesome."

I was realizing this even as I spoke the words. Unbelievable that I'd known Vi all these years and had never fully understood that being noticed wasn't her thing. How much time had I spent gabbing away about various things while she quietly listened? Or didn't listen . . . Either way, I hadn't been a very good friend to her.

"I'm sorry," I said.

My vision got all blurred and I realized my eyes were filling with tears. If I cried, people would probably wonder what was going on, but I didn't care. I wanted Vi to know what I was thinking.

"I'm not a very good friend," I said. "It's not even about the gossip. It's about how selfish I've been. I need to stop trying to be the center of attention."

"And I should learn to lighten up a little," Vi admitted. "Learn to not take things so seriously."

"Maybe that's what's always made us such good friends," I said. "We're so different."

"We balance each other out," Vi agreed. "I guess I just missed having you to talk to. You always had a crowd around you."

"I'm starting to realize that isn't really a good thing," I said. "Especially when they're only around to hear bad things about other people."

I should have known better in the first place. I'd gone from being Fatty Maddie in second grade to being the girl who talked about other people. Oh, sure, I didn't make fun of them to their faces like people had done to me, but was saying it in private any better? If I made fun of Kimmy Welles's big feet, for instance, even if she never heard it, wasn't it almost as bad?

"You're both being ridiculous," Jessica told us. I turned around to see that Sydney had joined us. She was covered in paint from head to toe. I looked down and realized I had quite a few paint spatters myself. When had that happened?

The two of them started giggling about something, leaving me to talk to Vi. There was an awkward silence, but Vi ended it.

"I guess I should tell you," Vi said. "Travis Fisher and I have talked."

She said it quietly, so no one else could hear. I had to hold in a squeal.

"Really?" I whispered. "When?"

"Yesterday afternoon. He stopped by my locker and asked me about my design."

I felt at least a little better about telling him about Vi liking him. But still . . .

"I know I messed up," I admitted. "I feel really bad. You know I was just trying to help by telling Travis what I told him."

It was hard to believe I'd given away a secret that huge. Best friends didn't tell things like that. There were some things you kept secret until the day you died.

"That's okay," she said. "I overreacted. But there are some things we still need to talk about."

I nodded. This wasn't the time or place. Even if we talked, things would probably be a little weird between us for a while. I'd have to keep my mouth shut and she'd have to—

There was nothing she'd have to do. I was the one who

needed to grow here. Although Vi had already realized that she needed to learn to have fun every now and then. Maybe smile, join in on the conversation, talk about something besides schoolwork . . .

"So, anyway," Vi said, raising her voice a little. "Jilly said during lunch they'll paint two parallel lines above the yellow part of the wall. We'll be allowed to paint whatever we want between those two lines. No approval needed."

"That's awesome," Jessica said. "What else did she say?"

It took me a second to figure out why this was so weird. I couldn't believe it, but Vivienne Lakewood—the girl who just recently told me that if I didn't have anything nice to say, I should keep quiet—was actually . . .

Gossiping?

Okay, so it was good gossip. It wasn't hurting anyone else. As I watched Vi's face light up, I realized it was completely possible to tell people news without hurting anyone else or breaking a trust. I smiled. Maybe I could still gossip. I just had to learn the difference between good gossip and bad gossip.

"She said they're picking the winner of the Hollywood trip after lunch," Vi continued.

"Wait," Jessica said, looking over at me. "Is Vi . . . *gossiping?*"

Since those were the exact words I'd just been thinking, I flashed a smile at Jessica. "Sometimes it's okay to gossip, right?" I asked Vi.

"Right," she said, surprising me. I'd been thinking it, but I didn't know she'd so easily admit to it. "Sometimes you're just sharing news."

"And sometimes it's good news," I added.

Vi turned to me. "I guess I was a little over the top," she said. "Besides, without you, I wouldn't have had the chance to meet my idol."

"Maybe you'll win?" Jessica asked hopefully.

"You could go to Hollywood," I added. I wasn't sure about the rest of it. From what I remembered, the person would be helping to host the show. Since Vi didn't want to be on TV, the "trip to Hollywood" part was the only thing that would appeal to her.

"The trip includes a day with the interior designers," Vi said. "It would be amazing."

"Plus, you'd be on TV." Sydney had missed the earlier part of our conversation, when it came out that Vi didn't like being on TV.

"Yeah, hopefully I can talk them out of that if I win." Vi looked nervous.

Jessica gasped. She looked at me. I knew that look. It

was, *How could anyone not want to be on TV? Is she crazy?*

I thought about it for a second. Camera in your face, the pressure to get every single word right . . . I could see why someone wouldn't want to be on TV. *I* wasn't one of those people—being on TV would be awesome—but I could see why she wouldn't like it.

Whatever happened, I had a feeling Vi was going to win the trip to Hollywood. She had to. There was nobody better at design than she was.

Chapter Fifteen

WE RETURNED FROM LUNCH TO FIND THE FLOOR WAS being ripped up. A team of men were doing it, and it looked fun. But they wouldn't let any of us have anything to do with it.

While they worked, we were allowed to start painting at the front of the hall. That left most of us standing around while the camera crew gathered around the small group of people painting stencils between those two yellow lines. I took some pictures, but I still felt like I should be doing something more productive.

That was when Jilly showed up.

"Are we ready to go work on the break area?" Jilly asked the group. She was looking at Vi, though.

"Me?" Vi asked.

"Yes." Jilly was beaming. Miss Golden stepped up next

to her and held up a page that looked like the pages in Vi's sketch pad. "Vi just showed me one of her designs. I'd like to work through some ideas with her. Anyone who would like to help can come on back."

Since we had nothing else to do, of course the entire group took off after Jilly. The camera crew, realizing this was where the action was, rushed after us. Someone had cleared the empty classroom completely out, leaving nothing but the old tile floor and plain white walls.

It was just like on TV. Jilly stood in the center of the room, talking to Vi about the overall vision. Vi was awesome, speaking just like the other people on reality shows. She sounded like an expert. I'd never been prouder of my BFF.

"Let's go," Jilly said. I wasn't sure what we were doing, but it all sort of fell into place. I had a feeling this would be the point in the show where they fast-forwarded and made us look like we were doing everything really fast. That was one of the few parts I always watched.

In real life, it didn't go at all like that. We painted and laid down a giant rug to cover the ugly floor. Then we watched while the muscular guys brought in a bunch of furniture, and Jilly and Vi rearranged it seven or eight times. By the end of it, I was standing next to Travis Fisher, watching him as he stared at Vi in amazement.

"She came up with all this," he said.

I nodded. "She's really smart."

He didn't say anything else. He didn't have to. He wandered around after her with wide eyes. By the time Miss Golden stood up in front of all of us to announce the winner, I was sure he liked her.

"I'm sure by now you've all seen the new break room," Miss Golden announced. The cameras weren't on anymore, and I assumed that was because this part wouldn't be shown. "You all have one person to thank for that. Vivienne Lakewood. Vivenne, come on up here. You're going to Hollywood!"

Everyone clapped, but Jess, Syd, and I clapped the loudest. Maybe it was my imagination, but a few people seemed like they weren't clapping very loudly. I looked around and saw Chelsea and friends. They were lightly clapping, while whispering to one another. They didn't look happy, especially Chelsea.

My gaze swept around farther. Other people were only half smiling as well. Meanwhile, Vi was walking up to the front of the crowd, a huge smile on her face. This was her moment. Everyone else could be jealous all they wanted, but it wouldn't change the fact that Vi had won. Vi was going to Hollywood!

"Thank you," Vi said, taking the envelope Miss Golden

handed to her. Jilly was on the other side of her. I pulled out my phone and started snapping photos. "I just wanted to thank my best friend, Maddie. Without her, I wouldn't be up here now. We have our . . . differences, but I couldn't have asked for a better friend. Thank you, Maddie."

I'd lowered my phone to stare at her, so now everyone could see my face as I blushed five different colors. I didn't feel like I deserved this. I'd been a bad friend, and even a trip around the world wouldn't completely make up for it. I'd just have to work hard every day to prove to Vi that I could stop gossiping.

It wouldn't be easy, but I had a feeling the key was to focus more on me and less on what everyone else was doing. In other words, I needed to *get a life*. Get some hobbies. Find something else to talk about besides Chelsea and Emma and Aiden and everyone else at this school.

"In that envelope, you'll find two round-trip tickets to LA," Jilly said. "You'll be spending three full days with the *24-Hour Makeover* crew, and, best of all, you'll help host the show."

I could tell from watching Vi that they'd had her all the way up to that last part. Her smile fell slightly, but she held it together. I was so worried, I began to make my way toward the front of the room as Jilly made final announcements.

The other kids began walking toward the door, but I kept

going in the other direction. I wasn't the only one. People were gathering around, trying to talk to Jilly, but I didn't care about Jilly. I wove around her and the line of people in front of her to sneak in behind Vi and Miss Golden.

I was all prepared to argue that Vi didn't really have to be on TV. They could just edit together the things she'd said here and let her work behind the scenes. But it was none of my business. That was how I'd gotten in trouble the first time—trying to help Vi in my way, instead of letting her figure it out a bit first.

"No problem," Miss Golden said. "In fact, we may have what we need from the conversations we've had during the course of the day today."

I felt a little panicked at that. Would they decide they didn't need her to come to Hollywood after all?

"What we may have you do," Miss Golden began, making my heart skip a beat, "is sit down with one of our producers, maybe even me, and talk about the experience and what you go through when you design. It would be an informal pretaped interview. Could you do that?"

Vi nodded, although she still looked a little uncomfortable. I wondered if she was thinking the same thing I was thinking. *Don't blow it, Vi. This is your chance to go to Hollywood and hang out with all your idols.*

"And this young lady over here is amazing." Miss Golden suddenly turned her gaze on me.

I didn't realize she'd known I was standing there, eavesdropping. I looked down, ashamed at having been caught.

But Vi wasn't mad I was listening. In fact, she turned to face me.

"She is," Vi agreed.

"Because of her, we had all of this turnout," Miss Golden added. "I can't believe Mr. Shelly thought that was a liability. You, young lady, have a future in PR."

I held my breath as I looked at Vi. What if Miss Golden's words reminded her why she was mad at me? Vi looked over at me and I couldn't read her expression, really, but I didn't want to take the chance of making her mad again, so when Miss Golden turned to talk to someone else, I rushed to make things right.

"Sometimes gossip can be good, right?" I asked. "I mean, I know it's bad to spread bad things about people, but what about things like this, where you want people to know something is going on so they'll help out?"

But even as I spoke, I could tell Vi wasn't mad. She looked thoughtful. I wondered if she'd been thinking the same thing.

"Miss Golden's right," Vi said, smiling. "You just might have a future in PR."

While we were on the subject, I wanted to get something out so it wasn't secret anymore. "I know you asked Syd to keep an eye on me," I admitted.

"I'm sorry," Vi said. "I shouldn't have had your own friend spy on you. I figured you'd get on the phone with Sydney and Jessica without including me, like you always do. So I had to make sure one of them was on board. I trust Sydney. She told me you weren't gossiping at all."

"I wasn't," I insisted. But something she'd said bugged me. "I always try to include you. I call you just as much as I call the two of them."

"But you talk to them about all kinds of things you don't talk to me about."

I saw it then. The hurt in her eyes. This was something that had been bothering her for a while. Why hadn't I seen it? Sure, Vi was antigossip and she believed in talking only about positive things, but that meant I shared stuff with Syd and Jess that I could never share with her. When I'd betrayed her trust with Travis, that had been the final straw.

"Not anymore," I said. "You come first. They can gossip if they want, but the gossip queen has closed up shop."

"Not completely." Vi held up her hand to stop me. "I think I know of a way you can use your talents for good."

Chapter Sixteen

One Troy Middle School seventh grader will see all her dreams come true next month when she travels to Hollywood to appear on *24-Hour Makeover*. Vivienne Lakewood, known to most of us as Vi, won the opportunity when the show spent a day helping us redo the language arts wing. Today Vi talks to us about her interior design work and how she feels about traveling across the country.

"Well? What do you think?"

Vi set down the piece of paper and looked at me. I hadn't realized I was holding my breath until that very moment.

Slowly, her face broke out into a smile. "I love it," she

said. She handed it to Sydney, who was quietly munching on a baby carrot.

"Where's the rest?" Sydney asked after reading the paragraph.

"We haven't done the interview yet," I said. Sydney handed the paper to me. "Vi has to come over to my house today after school."

"Or we could just do it here," Vi suggested.

Vi had been sitting with us at lunch since the day of the show—an entire week and a half. Day after day I'd stayed far, far away from gossip. But the need to let everyone know what was going on was still there, lurking beneath the surface.

That was why Vi's idea was perfect. She'd suggested I start up a real school newspaper. So I went to my language arts teacher, and she agreed to sponsor it. We didn't really have the money for printing, so it would be an electronic newsletter, viewable from the school's website.

Now the goal was to give people a reason to read it. That was where Vi came in. She was the star of the moment. People wanted to know about her, but Vi didn't like the spotlight. The only way that could happen was through an article written by her best friend.

There was one person who probably wouldn't read

the interview. She breezed past just as I was tucking the paragraph about Vi back into my bag. Chelsea and friends couldn't seem to walk past Vi these days without making some kind of noise.

Today it was just a loud laugh and the three of them looking down at us. They prissed their way to their usual table. I wanted to say something, but I held it in. Sydney didn't.

"Jealous losers," Syd said. "I'm going over to say something."

"No," Jess said. "Don't start a scene."

"I've been thinking. . . ."

This came from Sydney again. We all turned to look at her.

She sighed and plunged in. "Okay, so I know Maddie's a new person now and doesn't gossip, but her newspaper would be a great way to get at Chelsea. I'm not saying she should gossip, but what if the newspaper had a column written by, you know, someone here at school who might know a little about what's going on . . . ?"

"A gossip column as part of the newspaper," Jess said. "It's brilliant. And I assume you'd be the one who wrote it?"

"Maybe, but I'm not talking about gossip," she corrected. "Just *observations*. Like, 'What Troy Middle School seventh-grade princess can't stand that another girl got picked to go to Hollywood over her? Little does she know, she was never in the running.'"

I laughed. Jessica did too, but hers came out as a snort. Vi remained silent.

Sydney's smile fell as she noticed Vi's stoic expression. "It was a stupid idea," Syd said. "Forget it. I just wanted to find some way to get back at them."

"It might shut them up, too," Jessica said. She was looking at Vi hopefully.

Vi shook her head. "No."

She was as calm as ever as she said that one simple word. I realized that I'd never respected my best friend more than I did at that very moment.

"They're jealous," I said, not taking my eyes off Vi as I spoke. "The best way to get back at them is to ignore them completely."

That brought a smile from Vi. I watched her for a second, amazed. Even though Vi still always did what was best, she'd lightened up a lot in the past week and a half. She no longer sat there, quietly drawing in her sketch pad. Instead, she participated in the discussion and had fun with us.

We'd lost Sarah the minute she and Aiden stopped being so weird and started hanging out together. Now they were inseparable, staring into each other's eyes and doodling each other's names in their notebooks. Kelsey was a little upset about it—and said a few nasty things—but it's okay, I guess. Kelsey would eventually find a new guy to like and everyone would be happy.

And speaking of liking guys, Vi and Travis were on the verge of something. Vi told everything only to me, with me promising to keep it supersecret, and I absolutely would. I don't know what happened, but at some point I started seeing that all that gossiping wasn't making people like me. It was making people listen to me, but that's it. True friends— friends like Vi and Jessica and Sydney—don't care *what* you say. They just want to hang out. Plus, surprisingly, once I started focusing on myself, I really did stop worrying about what everyone else was doing.

Still, I wanted to write the *Troy Tattler*. The difference was that now, instead of spreading rumors, I wanted to do something positive. I'd track Vi's success every step of the way. Let Chelsea and the rest of the haters worry about what *we* were doing for a change. We would have the last laugh after all.

Did you **LOVE** this book?

Want to get access to
great books for  **FREE?**

Join

Simon & Schuster
IN THE
booklloop

where you can

✗ Read great books for FREE! ✗

Get exclusive excerpts

Chat with your friends

Log on to join now!

everloop.com/loops/in-the-book